Secrets Come Home

Ettie Smith Amish Mysteries Book 1

Samantha Price

Chapter 1

"Why would you have to go to the reading of the will, Ettie?" Elsa-May stood behind her sister and dusted her shoulders.

"I don't know, but if Bishop John says to be there, then that's exactly what I'll do." Ettie pushed Elsa-May's hand away. "Enough, there's nothing on my dress."

"There are tiny pieces of lint all over you. And please tie the strings of your prayer *kapp* together." Elsa-May breathed out heavily. "You look untidy."

"Then I'll be untidy. Ever since you've gotten those new glasses you've been on a cleaning frenzy."

Elsa-May folded her arms over her chest. "Agatha's most likely left you something in the will. That's what it sounds like to me."

Ettie adjusted her prayer *kapp*, pushing some loose strands of her white hair underneath it. "I don't know about that, but then again, Agatha had

1

no family to speak of."

"Do you want me to come along?"

Ettie pushed her lips together. *"Nee, denke.* I've got Eli collecting me." Eli was the bishop's eldest son.

"What am I supposed to do by myself, then?"

Ettie turned and glared at her sister. They didn't have to go everywhere together, did they? It was bad enough that they shared the same house; they didn't have to be joined at the hip. "Knit like you usually do. Or you could water the vegetables for me before the sun gets too hot."

Elsa-May scoffed, sat down and picked up her knitting. "That's your job. You know how the insects like me."

A giggle escaped Ettie's lips. Elsa-May was right. For some reason the mosquitos and anything else that could sting or bite found their way to Elsa-May's ankles, while leaving Ettie well alone. "I won't be long. I'm guessing she left me that china set of hers. She noticed me admiring it recently and asked me if I'd like it when she died. I laughed and said I'd be gone long before she would. I never had any reason to wonder why she asked me if I wanted it. Do you think she knew she was going to die soon?"

Either not hearing or not listening, Elsa-May stared at her hands and then looked up at Ettie. "I won't be able to keep knitting very much longer. Do you see the size of the fingers on my right hand?" Elsa-May held out a hand to Ettie.

Ettie walked a few paces to get a close look. *"Jah,* it looks swollen or something. Did you get stung by a bee?"

Elsa-May frowned at her sister. "It's called arthritis, Ettie, and when you're as old as I am you'll know what it's like when you can't close your hand fully."

Ettie grabbed her coat off one of the pegs by the door. "Nonsense, I'm nearly as old as you, and I don't intend to get arthritis or anything of the kind. Didn't you hear that I just asked you a question and you ignored me?"

Elsa-May frowned. "What question?"

Ettie sighed. "I asked you if you thought that Agatha knew she was going to die soon."

"How could she possibly know something like that?"

Ettie pulled on her coat. "I thought it odd that she asked me if I wanted her china set, when she's much younger than I am – or was much younger, I should say. Or is she still younger than I?" Ettie sat down on the couch facing Elsa-May. "Do you count someone as a certain age when they're dead?"

Elsa-May looked up from her knitting. "Have Eli stop by the store on the way back, would you? I wouldn't mind some candy. We've run out again."

Ettie sighed once more. Elsa-May hardly listened to her. Now with Agatha gone, she had one less friend to talk to, and she did like to talk. "You know that stuff's not good for you. That's probably what the insects are attracted to, all that sugar you eat."

"Just have him stop, will you? It'll save me getting a taxi out later today."

Ettie shook her head at her sister. They didn't

have their own buggy anymore and taxis were an expense they could barely afford. They grew most of their own vegetables and lived as thriftily as they could. Elsa-May ate the candy far too quickly these days; Ettie was lucky to see one tiny piece. That was just one of the things that Ettie had to contend with when living with her sister. But still, nothing in life was perfect.

She and Elsa-May were now in their early eighties. They'd both lost their husbands many years ago, and after living on their own for years had sold their farms and moved in together.

Agatha was just one more friend in their community whom they'd lost recently. She died at home, of natural causes, the doctor had said.

Ettie hurried over to the front door, opened it and peered out; there was still no sign of Eli's buggy. "He's running late," Ettie said, more to herself than her sister.

"You know the young don't care about time like we do."

"That's true, but it's not like Eli to be late, and

he's not that young anymore." Ettie wondered why Elsa-May chose to respond to murmurs when she ignored direct questions.

"Get me some of those soft caramels, too. *Nee,* not the ones that are covered in chocolate, the ones that are firm. *Jah,* firm caramels."

"I'll try to remember, and I'll stop if Eli can spare the time." Ettie left the front door open and sat down to wait.

"Very well, but if he can't spare the time, and if you don't come back with them, you know I'll have to go out myself and get them, don't you?"

The sound of horse's hooves was music to Ettie's ears.

"That'll be him now," Elsa-May said.

Ettie sprang to her feet and headed for the door.

"Don't forget–"

"I won't," Ettie said before she closed the front door behind her and hurried over to Eli, who was waiting in his buggy.

"Sorry, Ettie," said Eli. "I had a problem with

the buggy wheel. I had to change buggies at the last minute."

"What happened?" Ettie asked as she climbed into the passenger seat.

"I'm not sure – I'll have a better look at it when I get back home."

"Denke for driving me to town, Eli."

"Anytime, Ettie. You know that."

"Do you know who else is going to be there?"

Eli looked over at her. "In the lawyer's office?"

Ettie nodded.

"Dat didn't say. He just asked me to bring you. He's going to be there because he is a trustee of Agatha's estate. He couldn't take you there himself because he had things to do before and after seeing the lawyer."

"I understand. I could've got a taxi. Isn't it unusual for a lawyer to work on a Saturday?"

"I can't answer that, Ettie. I don't know too many lawyers."

Ettie pressed her lips together and wondered if she should write a will. When she sold the farm, she gave her children most of the money to help them toward buying places of their own, so she didn't have much left. She only had the house she shared with Elsa-May. That, she'd surely have to leave to Elsa-May because what good would it be to her children to have half a house? They wouldn't be able to sell it and leave their aunty Elsa-May homeless.

"You're awfully quiet today, Ettie."

Ettie gave a low chortle. "I'm getting closer to going home to be with *Gott,* and all my friends are leaving before me. Agatha was only sixty."

"Gott knows we want you to be here for a long time, Ettie."

The buggy stopped and Ettie looked to her side. "We're here already?"

"Jah, we are. When you get out, I'll move the buggy and park it in the parking lot around the corner. Do you need help to get down?"

"A hand would be good." Ettie hated needing help. Eli got out of the buggy and headed around to Ettie's side. "I'd hate to fall. Delma fell last winter and ended up in the hospital for six months. I have an extreme dislike for hospitals after a particularly bad experience a couple of years ago when I had pneumonia."

"I remember you were in the hospital for a time." Eli held her arm and released her when she was solidly on two feet. "There you are. I'll be waiting for you just around the corner there." Eli pointed in a northerly direction.

"Jah, I do recall you said that a minute ago. I might be old but I haven't lost my mind." She looked at Eli, hoping he hadn't taken offense. When she saw that he was smiling she added, "I'll see you soon, then. And after that, on the way home, do you think we could stop by the store? Elsa-May has asked me to get a few things for her."

"Of course."

Chapter 2

Ettie stood in front of the red brick building and stared up at it as a wave of heat from the pavement swept over her. She fanned her face with her hand. She could see from the signage in the window that Andrews Lawyers was one flight up. One flight of stairs would be no problem as long as there was a handrail. She was most likely the last one to arrive, so she hurried on in.

When she found the office, she pushed the glass door open and was pleased to be surrounded by cool air from the air-conditioning, a luxury she rarely enjoyed. She walked further in and stood in front of a red-haired receptionist.

"Are you Mrs. Ettie Smith?"

"I am."

"Everyone's in Mr. Andrews' office now." The receptionist rose to her feet. "Follow me."

What Ettie had thought was a cream pullover that the woman was wearing, she now saw was a slim-fitting dress. Ettie followed the lady and studied her hair. *How can she make it stand so tall on her head like that? Would hairspray alone be able to hold it? And her hair has to be colored artificially; no one has hair that color.*

The woman opened a door and said, "Mrs. Ettie Smith has arrived." She then stepped aside to allow Ettie through.

Ettie looked at the people in the room. The first person she saw was her Amish bishop who then introduced her to Mr. Andrews. Mr. Andrews was older than she'd expected, around sixty years of age, thin with large, black, heavy-framed glasses. She already knew Ava Glick, a young woman from the community.

Ettie took the spare seat next to the bishop. The lawyer's office was as she'd thought it would be, given the exterior of the building. The furniture was dark and heavy, and dark wallpaper lined the walls behind the bookcases, which were heavily laden with books.

"We should begin," the lawyer said.

"Sorry I'm late. There was a problem with one of Eli's buggies."

"It's quite all right," Mr. Andrews said. "We're all here now." He glanced at his watch. "I could read out the will, but to sum things up and for the sake of time, I'll tell you what she left to each of you." The lawyer looked at Ava and then Ettie. "I'm sure you're anxious to find out."

Ettie pushed her bottom lip out. There were only the two of them? Surely there would be more people Agatha would have left things to since she had no family. She had many friends.

"Mrs. Smith, Agatha King left you her house, all of its contents, and fifteen thousand two hundred dollars."

Ettie's hand flew to her mouth in shock. "There must be some mistake. Her whole house?"

"That's right, Ettie," the bishop said. "There's no mistake been made; I was there and witnessed the will when she signed it."

"There are conditions," the lawyer continued. "She has requested that you allow Ava Glick to continue to lease the apartment adjoining your house for the same sum she's paying now." He took his glasses off and looked directly at Ettie. "Legally, it's not a 'condition'; no one can enforce that on you. What she meant was that she would like you to do that. She'd like you to allow Ava Glick to continue living there as long as she wishes."

"Yes, of course." Ettie smiled at Ava and Ava's blue eyes crinkled at the corners when she smiled back. Agatha had mentioned finding someone to lease the *grossdaddi haus,* but who had leased it had never come up in their conversations.

"And Ava, Agatha King left you the sum of five thousand two hundred dollars and fifty six cents."

The young woman gasped. "Oh, that was so kind of her. I don't know what to say. I can't even thank her."

"I can't believe it at all." Ettie sat there stunned with her hand covering her mouth. The next thing she knew was that everyone was looking at her.

"That's it then, Ettie. You have a house, another house," the bishop said.

Ettie saw the bishop stand and realized it was time to go.

"I don't know what to say." She pushed herself to her feet.

"One more thing," the lawyer said as he rose from behind his desk. He opened a drawer and picked up a set of keys. "You might as well take these now. The papers will take some weeks to process, but the place is as good as yours. I'll try and push it all through quickly for you. There are going to be some charges for the transfers. Would you like me to take that out of the money she left you?"

"Yes, please do that." Ettie put her hand out for the keys. "Thank you." She stared down at the bunch. There must have been twenty keys tied together on a rope. It was just like her thrifty friend to buy a quality china tea set and save money on something trifling like a keychain.

"We're neighbors now, Mrs. Smith. You're my new landlord."

Ettie smiled at the young woman who she guessed

was in her mid twenties. "Call me Ettie, everyone does." Quite surprised by her friend leaving her so much, the next thing she was aware of was walking down the stairs. When Ettie reached the front of the building, Ava was nowhere to be seen. Ettie made her way to Eli's buggy and told him what had happened.

Before they got too far away from the lawyer's office, Eli said, "You had to stop by the store, Ettie?"

"*Jah,* the store. *Denke* for reminding me. I need to get some important things for Elsa-May."

An hour later, Ettie burst through the front door of the house she shared with her sister. Elsa-May was right where she'd left her. "Elsa-May, you'll never guess–"

"Wait! Did you get my candy?" Elsa-May lowered her knitting into her lap.

Ettie handed her the bag of candy and waited until Elsa-May had a piece in her mouth before she continued. "Agatha left me her *haus,* everything in it, and some money."

16

"Really? She left everything to you?"

Ettie nodded. "Mostly – she left some money to Ava Glick. "

Elsa-May screwed up her nose as she unwrapped another sweet. "Who?"

"You know, Ava – Joel and Karen's eldest *dochder.*"

"Ach, I know."

"Agatha requested that I let her live there as long as she wants in the *grossdaddi haus.*"

Elsa-May stared into the bag of candy. "Well, that sounds good."

"Did you hear me?"

"Jah, let Ava stay in the *grossdaddi haus.*" Elsa-May looked up at Ettie and the bag of candy fell into her lap. "Wait! You're not going to move into Agatha's *haus,* are you?"

Ettie sat on the couch. "I don't see why not. With the money she left me, and the rent coming in from Ava, I'd be able to afford the upkeep of it."

Elsa-May's shoulders drooped. "Would you leave me here all alone?"

Ettie hadn't thought the whole thing through. Was she supposed to invite Elsa-May to live with her? The two of them under the same roof in the small house had been fine for a time, but as the years wore on they were getting on each other's nerves more and more. Ettie longed for some peace and quiet without her sister's constant jibes and niggles. "I don't know what I'll be doing yet." Ettie looked down at the keys in her hand.

"Those the keys?" Elsa-May asked.

"Jah."

"Let's go and have a look at the place."

"What, now?"

"Jah."

Ettie frowned. "We'd have to get a taxi and that would eat into our weekly budget."

"Didn't you just say you inherited money?"

A smile tugged at the corners of Ettie's lips. They'd no longer have to be careful of every dime. "I'll call the taxi."

Ettie hurried outside and called the taxi from the phone in the shanty outside the Millers' house a few doors down. The Millers let everyone in the street use it, and the money for the calls was placed in a jar and was collected by Mr. Miller every few days.

Chapter 3

A waft of warm, stale air flowed over Elsa-May and Ettie as they pushed open the front door of Agatha's old house. The place smelled of dust and mold.

"Open some windows, Ettie."

Ettie made her way around to the windows in the living room. "It's surprising how musty it can get in such a short time. Agatha's funeral was a week ago, and the *haus* couldn't have been closed up for more than a fortnight." After she opened the windows, Ettie placed her hands on her hips. "Just as she left it."

"I wouldn't know; I haven't been here in a while," Elsa-May said as she too looked around the living room.

Ettie narrowed her eyes. "I just said it is. I wasn't asking you anything."

"No need to snap at me," Elsa-May said.

"I wasn't. I was simply saying that the place

looks just the same."

"Well, why wouldn't it?"

Ettie shook her head and said nothing more. She caught sight of Agatha's rocking chair and walked over to it. "And here's her chair." She ran her fingers over the wood on the top rail of the rocking chair.

"It's her *haus* – why wouldn't her chair be in it?"

"It's my house now." Ettie gave a little giggle knowing her sister couldn't argue with that. She pictured her dear friend still alive and sitting in the chair.

"That's just what I need, a rocking chair." Elsa-May pushed past Ettie and sat in Agatha's chair. As she did, something on the floor caught her eye. She leaned forward to pick it up.

"What is it, Elsa-May?"

"I thought it was little bits of dirt, but it appears you might have woodworm or something of the sort."

Ettie leaned down to have a look. There were small holes in the floorboards. "It looks as though something's been eating it. It might be white ants."

"I'll have Jeremiah come and take a look."

"Denke, that would be good, and while he's here he can see what else needs to be done. The whole place looks rundown."

"We can go straight to his place now. These things shouldn't be left too long."

Ettie nodded and hoped she hadn't been left a liability. What if the whole house was infested with white ants and was about to fall down? It was convenient that her great nephew, Jeremiah, was a builder and lived so close.

* * *

Elsa-May led her grandson into the house and showed him the holes that concerned them.

"It's not looking good." He knocked on the floor. "They've been eaten through." He knocked on the surrounding boards. "It seems to be just these few here, which is odd."

"Why is that odd?" Elsa-May asked.

"These boards appear to be made of different wood from the rest of the floor. I'd say there would have been some repair at some stage on the house and they've used a softer wood."

"Can you fix it?" Ettie asked.

Jeremiah looked up at Ettie from his crouched position. "I've got some boards in my barn that are pretty close to these others." He nodded toward the good floorboards. "If it's only those few boards that need replacing, I should be able to do it tomorrow. Oh, tomorrow's Sunday – I'm glad *Gott* tells us to have a day of rest. I'll do it first thing Monday."

"Okay, please do it," Ettie said.

"If you aren't in a hurry, I can get my tools out of the wagon and make sure it's only these few. Then I'll get under the house with a flashlight and have a look."

Ettie looked at Elsa-May.

"We're in no hurry," Elsa-May said.

Ettie nodded. "That would be excellent, Jeremiah."

Jeremiah headed out to his wagon and Elsa-May and Ettie sat down.

"This wasn't what I expected when I came over here," Ettie said.

"Best you know so you can get it fixed."

"What if they start eating the rest of the *haus?*"

"I'll ask Jeremiah; there's surely some way to treat them to ensure that they go and don't come back."

"I'll make us a cup of tea." Ettie headed to the kitchen, and when she got there she looked out the window. Jeremiah was talking to Ava. *Ah, they're about the right age for one another.* Ettie giggled as she remembered what it was like to be young and carefree. She took her mind off days gone by and put the pot on the stove. When she sat back down next to Elsa-May, she heard noises underneath their feet, indicating that Jeremiah was under the house.

Ten minutes later, Jeremiah came back inside. "I think we need to call the police."

"Why, what's the matter?" Ettie wondered if the house violated some kind of building code, but if so, why did the police need to get involved?

"There's a body under the house." Jeremiah pulled his hat off his head.

"A *dead* body?" Elsa-May asked as she made her way to stand beside Ettie.

Jeremiah nodded. "A dead *person*."

Elsa-May and Ettie stared at each other. Who would they call, now that their old friend Detective Crowley had retired?

Elsa-May looked back at Jeremiah. "Do you know who it is?"

He shook his head. "A man. Looks as though he's been dead for some time. He's wrapped up tight in plastic and covered in a blanket or rug of some sort."

Elsa-May grimaced. "Are you sure it's a man?"

Jeremiah scratched his chin. *"Nee.* I just assumed, that's all."

"Well, you go and call the police then, Jeremiah. We'll wait here," Elsa-May instructed.

Ettie and Elsa-May stared at each other again. If the man was wrapped in plastic, he'd been murdered for certain.

* * *

Half an hour later, an ambulance, police cars with flashing lights, and a detective were outside the house.

"Are you coming outside, Ettie?" Elsa-May asked over her shoulder as she went to have a closer look.

Ettie shook her head. *"Nee.* I'll wait here."

When Elsa-May was out of the house, Ettie peeped out the window to see Elsa-May already speaking to a detective. She sat down to the sound of banging and scraping from underneath the house as the crowd's chatter hummed in the background. Would she feel comfortable moving into this house knowing that a dead body had been under the floor? She wondered how long the body had been there. *Who could the dead person be?*

Chapter 4

Ettie couldn't bring herself to go out and watch what the police uncovered. A small crowd of neighbors and the press had gathered. When the ambulance took the body away, Elsa-May joined Ettie inside the house.

"Let's go home, Ettie."

Ettie looked up at Elsa-May. "What did they find?"

Elsa-May took a deep breath. "It was a man. They don't know who he is at this stage. From his clothing, it looks like he was Amish. The body's been taken to the morgue to be examined. They'll try to identify him. He had no wallet or anything on him – nothing."

"Why was he here?" Ettie turned to look at the floorboards that had led to the grisly discovery.

Elsa-May followed Ettie's gaze, and said, "Jeremiah said he was directly under those boards."

Ettie's mouth fell open. "That's right where

Agatha sat; he was right underneath her feet."

"It seems so." Elsa-May slowly nodded.

"Is Jeremiah ready to go?"

"*Jah,* the detective's finished talking to him."

"Who's the detective?" Ettie asked.

"He's a young man, Detective Kelly. Keith Kelly, I believe he said."

"Have we met him before?" Ettie asked.

Elsa-May shook her head. "I don't think so. He's not been in the area long. He's Crowley's replacement."

"It'd be good if Crowley was still around. He was so helpful."

"Sometimes he was and sometimes he wasn't. He wasn't always eager to help when we needed it," Elsa-May reminded Ettie.

Ettie stated, "He always came through in the end if I remember correctly."

"Hmm." Elsa-May pressed her lips into a thin line, and then said, "I'm certain he wouldn't mind if we called him and told him about the dead man under the floor of your new *haus.*"

Ettie shook her head. "There's no reason. I'm sure Detective Kelly will be able to wrap things up without Crowley's help. Let him have his retirement in peace."

* * *

It was Monday when Elsa-May and Ettie got a visit from Detective Kelly. Elsa-May answered the door. "Ettie, it's the detective I told you about. The one who took over from Crowley." She looked back at him. "Come in and have a seat."

The detective walked a few steps into their living room and sat on one of their rickety wooden chairs. "You two ladies knew Detective Crowley?"

"Yes, we did," Elsa-May answered before Ettie had a chance.

The detective turned his attention to Ettie. "You knew Agatha King well?"

Ettie's heart pitter-pattered at a quicker rate. The man wasn't a bit like Crowley, this man was much younger and seemed not nearly as friendly.

"Yes, very well. We both knew her; she's part of our Amish community." *If only Crowley were still around.*

"She left you her house, I understand, Mrs. Smith?"

Ettie nodded.

"Did you find out who that poor man was, Detective?" Elsa-May asked.

"He was Horace Hostetler."

Ettie and Elsa-May gasped and looked at each other.

The detective leaned forward. "You knew him?"

Ettie nodded. "He disappeared many years ago. Horace and Agatha nearly married some years back."

"Many years ago." Elsa-May put her hand to her head. "I had a dreadful fear that it might be Horace."

Ettie looked at her sister and frowned. "You never mentioned that to me."

Elsa-May looked at Ettie and remained silent.

The detective made a sound in his throat, and

then pulled a notepad out of his pocket. He looked up at Ettie. "When was the last time you saw him?"

Ettie ignored his question, and asked, "How do you know it was Horace? I heard that there wasn't much left of the body."

"His mother reported him as a missing person some years ago. We had his dental records on file from that time. We knew the body was dressed in Amish clothing and we don't have many reports of missing Amish men, so it didn't take as long to connect the dots."

"But he went missing when he was on *rumspringa*. So he wouldn't have been in Amish clothing," Ettie said.

"Well, Ettie, he could have just come back to the community, like we'd heard, and been killed then," Elsa-May said.

The detective raised his hand. "In or out of the community, it doesn't matter to me. Neither do the clothes he was wearing when he was murdered, except for the fact it enabled us to speed our identification of him." The detective looked between the two of them. "Now, I shall ask you again, Mrs. Smith – when was the last time you saw Horace Hostetler?"

"It was many years ago, Detective. I'd say that Agatha would've been just a girl, nearly a young woman."

"That's right, they had both left the community and Agatha returned. They were to marry before they left, and then Horace came back, but he left again suddenly. Is that how it happened, Ettie?"

"From memory, I think that's correct. I know they both left around the same time. They were going to marry, then they just up and left the community before they did, and only Agatha returned."

Elsa-May chimed in. "Obviously he'd come back or he wouldn't have been in those clothes."

The detective frowned. "They left the Amish together, then? Agatha came back, followed by Horace, and then Horace suddenly left again?"

"I had heard Horace would return and they'd continue with their plans of marriage, but he never did. Now, hearing about the clothing, it appears he did return and then he must have been murdered straight away," Ettie said.

"Could you both please keep your answers to the point?" The detective raised his eyebrows and scribbled something in his notebook. He looked up at them. "Did they get along well, Agatha and Horace?"

"As well as any couple who were going to get married," Elsa-May answered.

"Why do you ask, Detective? You don't suspect that Agatha had anything to do with his death, do you?" Ettie asked as she leaned forward.

He stared at Ettie and blinked a couple times. "Well, the man was murdered. He was found under her floor. When we have a murder, the first person we look at is the spouse – or, as in this case, the significant other. When you put two and two together, Mrs. Smith, you wind up with four."

"But not always," Ettie said before she could stop herself. When the man frowned at her she realized what she'd said. "I mean, two and two make four, of course they do. Well, except if you draw a two, and then you draw another two, and then two and two make twenty two. Very often the most likely or the obvious answer is not…"

As Ettie struggled to finish her sentence, Elsa-May chimed in. "What Ettie is trying to say is that it's a ridiculous notion to think that Agatha was capable of hurting anyone. No one in our community would be capable of doing such a thing – that's my opinion. I suggest, Detective, that you start looking outside the community for your murderer."

Worried that they were getting on the wrong side of the man, Ettie changed the subject slightly. "How was Horace killed, might I ask?"

"A blow to the back of the head. Looks like it came from a broad, flat object. As there wasn't any flesh left, the coroner could only gather evidence from the skeletal remains."

Ettie grimaced at the image his words conjured up.

"Have you spoken to Horace's family?" Elsa-May asked.

"They've been informed, but they haven't been formally questioned yet."

Ettie scratched her chin. "I guess that explains why they've not heard from him in years."

"Tell me, Mrs. Smith, did Agatha ever marry?"

"No, she didn't."

The detective continued, "Did she have any gentleman friends who might have been jealous of Horace's attention toward her?"

Ettie stared into the distance and rubbed her top lip with her index finger while she thought. "If she did, I didn't know about them."

"Well," Elsa-May added. "That means 'no' because Ettie is the one person who always knows what's going on in our community. She talks to everyone – she's friends with everyone and she's always talking."

"You're making me sound like a gossiper, Elsa-May, and I'm not."

"You do talk with everyone."

Ettie frowned. "Not everyone, I don't."

The detective stood up. "Well, thank you, ladies.

I might have some more questions for you at another time."

Elsa-May and Ettie stood as well. "Anytime, Detective," Elsa-May said as she showed him to the door.

Ettie walked up beside her sister and they watched him get into his car. When the sisters were alone again, they sat down.

"He thinks Agatha had something to do with Horace's death." Ettie exhaled loudly.

"It certainly sounds that way."

"I wonder how he got under the floor like that. Who do you think did it, Elsa-May?"

"I don't know anyone that would have a reason to kill him, but we don't know what happened when he was on his *rumspringa*. Many a young man has gotten himself into trouble when he ran around with the *Englischers.*"

Ettie sighed. "She came back to the community without him."

"And that was after her *mudder* died and left her the *haus?*"

38

Ettie nodded. "Her *mudder* died when Agatha was sixteen, I remember that. It was always just the two of them with Agatha's *vadder* dying years before."

"How old was Agatha when Horace left?"

"She would've been eighteen and Horace would've been around the same age."

"And living in that place by herself?"

"Jah. What are you thinking?" Ettie asked her sister.

"It seems odd that a stranger would kill him and then put him under her *haus.* Wouldn't it have been easier to dump a body somewhere else rather than wrap the body and bury it under the *haus?"*

"Seems it was a good place to hide it. No one found it for forty years, and if it weren't for you spotting those holes in the floorboards, he might never have been found."

"Possibly." Elsa-May scratched her neck.

"You're not thinking Agatha did it, are you?"

"Don't you think it odd that her rocking chair was directly over the body? It's an odd place for a chair, to be placed in the middle of the room like that."

Ettie breathed out heavily and cast her mind back to her many visits with Agatha. She'd always considered it most strange for the rocking chair to be where it was, but then again Agatha did live alone. It wasn't as though she had to be mindful of others and keep the centre of the room clear. "That's what we have to do then, Elsa-May."

Elsa-May lowered her eyebrows and looked at Ettie over the top of her glasses. "What?"

"We have to find out from Jeremiah how the body would've got there."

"How would he know? He wasn't even alive back then," Elsa-May said before she realized what Ettie meant. "Oh, I see. Did the floorboards have to be taken up for the body to be placed where it was, or was the body simply dragged under the house? That would explain why those boards were different, perhaps."

"Exactly." Ettie nodded.

"It seems obvious to me that the boards were

taken up, but then the person would have had to have access to the *haus*. Well, we shall do that. First thing tomorrow we'll go and see Jeremiah."

That evening, as Ettie watered her vegetables, she cast her mind back to dredge up what she could remember about Horace and Agatha. Agatha and she weren't close back in those days. Agatha was a young single girl, and Ettie was busy with her own large family. She knew that Agatha had returned to the community, and had heard talk of Horace returning and that was all. Perhaps she should make her own enquiries with Horace's family. They'd know if Horace had spoken of having crossed or accidently wronged someone, and they might know if he'd had any enemies.

A smile crossed Ettie's face as she bent down to look at her tomato plants. The first tomato had formed. It was the size of a large cherry, and it was still green. "It's a wonder I didn't see that before," she murmured to herself. When she finished the watering, she placed the watering can by the back door. Elsa-May could be heard rattling around in the kitchen making dinner.

Ettie decided that when Elsa-May went to her Wednesday knitting circle, the day after tomorrow, she would visit Horace's family alone. If God willed it, they would find out more from Jeremiah tomorrow about how the body was placed. With that knowledge she could go to Horace's family with a little more information up her sleeve.

Chapter 5

Ettie and Elsa-May's taxi came upon Jeremiah's buggy just as he was leaving his house.

"Where are you two headed?" Jeremiah asked when the taxi drew even. "I could take you."

"We're coming to see you, but you could take us home and we can talk to you on the way," Elsa-May said.

"Fine." Jeremiah agreed.

After they paid the taxi driver, the two elderly ladies climbed into the buggy.

"What did you want to talk to me about?" Jeremiah clicked the horse onward.

"We were curious about the body," Ettie began.

"Jah," said Elsa-May. "How would it have been placed there? Would it have been lowered from above? You did say you thought that some of the floorboards were different from the others."

"What are your thoughts, Jeremiah?" Ettie asked.

"It could have been dragged under the *haus,*

but it's a tight fit and would've been hard to do. It would more likely have been lowered from above. And the boards there are different, but I'm not sure that's the reason. They could have still used the old boards. Lifted the boards up, lowered the body, and then nailed the boards back down."

"Would the boards normally be damaged when they lifted them up?" Ettie asked.

"Unlikely; not if someone knew what they were doing. It's not hard to lift some boards up," Jeremiah said.

"So the person who did it might have split the boards and had to replace them and that's why the boards are different?" Elsa-May asked.

Jeremiah rubbed his jaw. "It's straightforward – I don't think anyone would make a hash of lifting boards up."

"They were damaged somehow, and because the body was right underneath those replaced pieces of wood, it seems likely that's when it was done."

"*Jah*, it would be an extreme coincidence – the softer wood being directly over the body, and all,"

Jeremiah said.

"Precisely," Elsa-May commented. "So we can guess that the person who placed the body under the floor was not good at using tools."

"A woman perhaps?" Jeremiah said, causing the sisters to glare at him. He quickly added, "I mean to say, not all women can use tools, but I'm certain there are many that can."

* * *

As soon as Elsa-May's friend, Deidre, came to fetch her for the knitting circle, Ettie hurried along the road and called a taxi. She would go to her new house and gather her thoughts before she headed to Horace's mother's place.

The ride in the taxi was a fast one and no sooner had Ettie paid the driver and got out of the taxi than she saw Ava hurrying toward her.

"Ettie, I'm glad you're here."

The taxi sped away.

"What is it, Ava? You look dreadful."

"There was a man hanging around the *haus* last night. I heard some scratching noises, so I looked outside and saw a dark figure. I opened the door and called 'who's there' and he ran off."

"Did you see who it was?"

Ava shook her head.

"I called the police first thing this morning."

"What did they say?"

"They said if I'm scared I should get a dog or a personal alarm. That's after they found out I didn't have a telephone."

"What time did you see the man?"

"Around two. I couldn't sleep and when I got up I saw it was a few minutes past two. I went to light the lamp, but before I could, I saw someone over near the front corner of your *haus*. They were crouching down."

"The police didn't come out?"

Ava shook her head. "They might have if I'd been able to call them at the time. Agatha had always talked about getting a phone in the barn, but she never did anything about it. Do you know it's in the papers?"

"What – Horace's murder?"

"Jah, the story was in the paper yesterday. When I gave the police our address, the officer said it was in the paper."

Ettie tapped her fingers on her chin, wondering if the newspaper article had caused them the unwanted attention.

"You know the police think that Agatha did it?"

Ettie looked up at her. "I thought she was a suspect, but I didn't think they thought she was a killer. Surely not."

"I'm convinced of it. They asked me to go to the police station so they could ask me some questions."

"Did you go?"

"Yes, I went yesterday."

"What did they ask you?"

"They asked me what kind of things Agatha spoke to me about, how well I knew her, if I knew any of her close friends, and if she'd ever mentioned Horace."

"Had she ever mentioned Horace to you?"

"She had. She told me there's no right man and I shouldn't wait for one. I asked her how she knew and she told me about Horace and that he disappointed her – she thought she loved him. I'm sorry now that I didn't pay more attention to what she said."

"That's sad, very sad. She was waiting for him to come back and he never did. She would've thought he didn't love her when all the while he was right under her feet."

Ava nodded. "I guess it is sad when you look at it like that. Are you going to move in or are you thinking of selling?"

"I don't think I could sell. Agatha wouldn't want me to do that, not when she said she wanted you to stay. I was seriously thinking of moving in until all this happened."

"Please move in, Ettie. I'm a little scared now. It'd be nice to have you living close by."

"You're frightened?"

"More unnerved, I'd say. There's a dark, gloomy

feeling hanging over the place – Agatha's gone and now this discovery under the boards..."

"Do you want to come inside?" Ettie asked. "I can't stand for too long before I get tired."

"Okay."

Ettie and Ava walked into the house and sat down in the living room. "It's unfair that Agatha isn't here to clear her name," Ettie said.

"Nothing about the law is fair, Ettie. It's not fair that people who have no money are severely disadvantaged. Some people are in jail who wouldn't be there if they had money for bail. I heard of a man who was in jail waiting for a trial for three years and he was totally innocent – he just didn't have the money for bail."

"That is unfair."

"The world's justice system is unfairly slanted to disadvantage areas of... Oh, I'm sorry, Ettie; I'm sure you don't want to listen to my tirades."

"Nee, I do. I'm interested in what young people think."

Ava leaned forward. "I've done a few legal

studies. I got my GED and started college, without anyone in the community knowing. It was Agatha who encouraged me."

"I won't tell anyone," Ettie said wondering what Ava's parents would have to say on the matter.

"I didn't think you would." Ava giggled.

"What happened with your studies – you said you started?"

"It's not a practical thing to do. I don't want to leave the community; I struggled with what to do for a while, before I decided to stay. I thought I might be able to do a lot of good if I became a lawyer or maybe a case worker, but then Agatha pointed out that a person can do good wherever they are and whatever they're doing."

"That's true enough. She was a smart woman."

"It's a loss, for sure and for certain. She became a good friend," Ava said before giving a sigh.

"I never saw you around when I visited her."

"I kept in my *haus* when I saw she had visitors. We respected each other's privacy like that."

Ettie chortled. "You probably didn't want to get

stuck talking to old people."

"Nee, it's not that at all," Ava said.

Ettie slapped her hands together. "I was on my way to talk to Horace's *mudder* to see what I can find out."

"She's still alive?"

"Jah, she's Doris Hostetler. Horace's sister, Sadie, never married and she's still living at home."

"Jah, I know Doris and Sadie. I didn't realize they were related to the man who was killed. There are so many Hostetlers in the community. Can I come? I can drive you in my buggy to save you getting a taxi."

"That would be *wunderbaar; denke,* Ava. Keep your eyes and ears open. We have to find some clue that will help clear Agatha's name."

"I hope we do."

"Me too."

Chapter 6

When they approached the Hostetlers' place, Ettie saw Sadie sweeping the porch. "There's Sadie."

"How old would Sadie be?"

"She'd have to be sixty, and Doris, her *mudder,* is much older than I am – in her early nineties, I'd say."

"Sadie always looks so unhappy. In a scary kind of way."

"She does. She's a spinster and not to happy about it. She had two men she liked but they ended up marrying other women."

By the time they got out of the buggy, Sadie had disappeared.

Doris came to the front door and waited for them. "Ettie, Ettie." She reached out her hands toward her and Ettie took hold of them. "You heard?"

Ettie nodded. "I'm sorry, Doris."

"That's why he never came back. I always

wondered if I should've done or said something different – I always blamed myself. I never could have done anything about him not coming back. I feared something bad might have happened so I reported him to the police as a missing person some years back, but I still heard nothing." Doris looked over at Ava and then back to Ettie. "Elsa-May's not with you?"

"Nee, she's at a knitting circle. I'm afraid I didn't tell her I was coming here, but she'll visit soon, I'm sure. You know Ava, don't you?"

"Jah, I do. Morning, Ava."

"Good morning."

"Ava lives in Agatha's *grossdaddi haus."*

"I'd heard that. Come in, Sadie's got the pot boiling so we can have a nice cup of hot tea."

Doris had a tight grip on Ettie's arm as she pulled her inside.

After they made polite small talk, Doris informed them the funeral was set for the day after tomorrow, on Friday. "It will be a closed casket." The lines in Doris' face depended as she frowned and looked up at the ceiling.

"*Jah,* of course," Ettie said, thinking they could do it no other way. "Did the police say anything of who might have done it?"

Doris stared at Ettie for a without answering her, making Ettie regret her sudden question. Sadie placed a tray of tea and cookies on the small table in front of them and sat down. Ettie could see that Sadie was disturbed by her brother's death. She looked paler than she usually did and her cheeks were drawn in, almost as though she hadn't eaten anything or even had anything to drink in days. The dark grape-colored dress Sadie wore under her white apron did nothing to improve her complexion.

After everyone had a cup in hand, Doris eventually answered Ettie. "They consider that Agatha was the most likely person to have done it. I told them that was nonsense."

"I see," Ettie said before bringing the tea to her lips.

"Don't you think it nonsense, Ettie?" Doris

asked.

"I absolutely do, but do you have any idea who might have done it? He was on *rumspringa* at the time, I believe. Did he come back and visit you?"

Doris and Sadie exchanged glances. "He visited twice early on while he was still on *rumspringa*," Sadie said, contributing to the conversation for the first time.

"Did he talk of anyone – anyone who had cause to harm him?"

"He did have an argument with Agatha," Sadie said opening her blue-green eyes widely.

"He did?" Ettie asked.

Sadie nodded. "He said he was coming back to the community and went to tell Agatha, thinking she'd be happy, and they had a terrible row."

Doris scrunched up her nose.

"Did he tell you that?" Ettie asked.

Sadie nodded. "He came to say goodbye straight after he'd seen her, and told me they'd had a terrible argument. Then he told me he was going away for a long time, heading up north. Before he left, he said he'd go back and try to make amends with her just one more time. That was the last time I saw him."

"Did you tell the police that?" Ettie asked.

Sadie nodded.

"You've never told me that, Sadie," her mother said looking at her in disbelief.

"I didn't want to upset you, *Mamm.*"

"The police questioned us separately. I wondered why they thought Agatha did it. Now they think she did it because of what you said, Sadie."

"I had to tell the truth, didn't I?" Sadie scrunched up her face and looked as though she would cry.

Ettie couldn't imagine how hard it would be to have a sibling disappear, not knowing if they were dead or alive.

"Jah, of course you had to tell the truth," Doris said, trying to calm Sadie.

"You must have missed your *bruder* over all these years, Sadie," Ava said.

"They got on so well," Doris said.

"We all missed him," Sadie said before she gave

a sniffle.

"Did the police talk to the rest of your *kinner?*" Ettie asked Doris, trying to recall just how many children she had. She was certain it was six – or was it seven?

"They said they wanted to talk to them, and I gave the police all their addresses. They might have talked to them already."

"What about friends of Horace? Did you know any of Horace's *Englisch* friends?" Ava asked.

"There were two boys – well, men – he brought with him the second time he came here. He showed them the farm. I don't know their names now, but he said he worked with them."

"Doing what?" Ettie asked, hoping to have a lead.

"Building. Building new homes. It was a construction company."

"Do you remember the name of it?" Ava asked.

Doris looked at her daughter. "You'd remember it, Sadie; you've got such a good memory for names and such."

Sadie shook her head. *"Nee,* I don't remember."

Doris frowned at her. "We were talking about it just yesterday." Doris' gaze turned to the ceiling. "It was the name of a bird. Finch Homes? *Nee,* it wasn't that."

"Sparrow?" Ettie suggested.

"Wren?" Ava added.

"Nee, none of those. Starling, that's what it was Starling Homes. Wasn't it, Sadie?"

"That's right it was, *Mamm.* Starling Homes."

Doris took a sip of tea.

Sadie peered at Ettie. "Why are you asking all these questions, Ettie?"

"Agatha was a good friend and I want to clear her name."

Sadie asked, "How?"

"By finding out who killed your *bruder,"* Ettie added.

Doris leaned forward. "Perhaps you should leave things well alone, Ettie. He's gone and nothing will bring him back. No one in the community thinks that Agatha would do such a thing. Leave it well alone."

"What *Mamm* said is right, Ettie. He's gone; it won't bring him back."

Ettie shook her head. *"Nee,* I can't. I owe it to Agatha to clear her name. She'd want me to do that."

Ava turned to Sadie. "Was Starling Homes a local business?"

Sadie nodded. "It was, but I couldn't tell you where it was located."

* * *

Once they were in the buggy and driving away from the Hostetlers' home, Ava said, "That was interesting."

"Jah, it was. What part did you think was the most interesting?"

"I haven't had much to do with them, since they're so much older. I didn't know they'd be so nice and friendly."

Ettie shrugged her shoulders, wishing she'd

brought Elsa-May with her instead of Ava. Still, she was pleased she had someone with her. "Now we need to find out what we can about the building company Horace worked for."

"Are you going to talk to people Horace knew back then?"

"Jah. We can look it up in a phone book at the local store on the way home. Hopefully the firm will still be in business."

"Very good." Ava nodded.

Ten minutes later, Ava returned to the buggy with a phone number and address. "Excellent," Ettie said, staring at the contact details. "We should visit and find out who they employed all those years ago."

"Would they tell us that? Wouldn't they consider that private information? And wouldn't the police be doing all this?" Ava asked.

"That's a good question. Let's go and visit Detective Kelly right now and I'll ask where he's gotten with everything."

Chapter 7

"Ah, Mrs. Smith and Ms. Glick, have a seat," After they sat down opposite him, Ettie looked around the office. He was in Crowley's old office sitting behind Crowley's old desk. She glanced at a framed photograph on his desk. It was an attractive dark haired woman with a dog. "Is that your wife?" Ettie asked nodding her head to the picture.

The detective frowned and tilted the picture away from sight. "Have you come with any information regarding Horace Hostetler?"

"We were hoping you might have found something out. Ava drove me here to see you because I'm a little frightened of living in the house by myself. Do you know who killed him yet?"

"It's still under investigation, but it's looking more and more like a lovers' quarrel. I'm afraid it happens more than anyone would like to think. Things got a bit heated and without thinking Agatha whacked him over the head with a frying pan; then she panicked and hid him under the floor."

"Are you certain? Agatha was such a small woman and Horace was well over six feet. If he were standing, how would she reach his head? And if sitting, wouldn't he notice her moving around him with a frying pan in hand? How would she have managed to bind his body and then place him where he was?" Ettie said.

"As I said, Mrs. Smith, it's still under investigation. I think you'll be safe enough in the house; I'd say whoever murdered that man would be long gone."

"What about the prowler I saw last night?" Ava asked.

The detective raised his eyebrows forming lines in his forehead. "You had a prowler?"

"Yes, I called here early this morning. You weren't in and they said they'd pass the message along."

The detective studied Ava for a moment before he spoke. "No, I wasn't informed."

"I asked them to tell you about the person I saw because of what had happened. I told them about the body found under the house, and they said they'd heard about it."

"What happened – did we apprehend the trespasser?" Kelly asked.

Ava shook her head. "No one came out."

"Ava said that there's never been anything like that happen at the house since she's been living there. Do you think it's got something to do with the murder, Detective?"

He shook his head. "There's a small section of the population, the criminal element, who lurk around at night looking for harmless mischief. I can't see that it's related to your friend."

Ava and Ettie looked at each other, and then Ettie said, "Someone mentioned you were going to speak to Horace's family and friends from back then?"

"We're still trying to track down a few people." The detective's eyes fell to a scrap of paper on his desk. He picked it up and asked, "You don't happen to know a Terence Wheeler, do you?" He let the paper slide from his fingers back onto the desk.

Ettie pressed her lips together and her eyes flickered upward. "No, I can't say that I do. Was he a friend of Horace's?"

"We're not sure yet. It's a name we've heard a couple times during our investigations."

"He's not from the community," Ettie added.

"We know that much. Horace's family hadn't heard of anyone going by that name."

Ettie licked her lips. "Have you looked into the building company that Horace worked for?"

"Do you have some information that we don't know about?"

"No, I don't." Ettie's eyes were glued to the detective, waiting for his next response. "Unless you didn't know about that job."

"We've got no plans to, and we did know about that." Detective Kelly leaned back. "In a case like this, this old, it's unlikely his killer will be found unless we're lucky enough to find some tangible evidence." He placed his hands out, palms up. "So far we've got nothing."

"What about looking for enemies he might have had?"

The detective laughed. "Leave the detective work to us, Mrs. Smith."

"I just thought that–"

"I know what you're saying, Mrs. Smith, but if we had any reason to believe that there was a crazed killer on the loose we'd be on to it. I think we already have a good idea who killed the man, but we'll probably never be able to prove it." The detective pushed back his chair and stood up. "Now, if you ladies will excuse me, I've got work to do."

* * *

When they were outside the police station, Ava glanced at Ettie, who was staring down at her hands. "What are you thinking, Ettie? You've gone quiet."

"I just would've preferred it if the detective had treated us with respect."

"I know two reasons why he treated us that way."

"Jah, we're Amish and we're women," Ettie said with a glint in her eyes.

"Exactly." Ava laughed and then said, "Agatha couldn't have, and wouldn't have, hurt anyone in any way."

"We know that, but I don't think we've got any way of making the detective see it," Ettie said.

"Try not to get upset – we'll get to the bottom of things."

"Who do you think Terence Wheeler is?" Ettie asked.

Ava shrugged. "No idea. Are you moving into the house? I'd feel much safer if you were there."

"I shall. I'll stay there tomorrow night if that'll make you feel better. You're quite welcome to stay with me and Elsa-May tonight. We've only got a small *haus* but we have a comfortable couch."

"Nee denke, Ettie. I'll be all right. I'll sleep with a light burning."

"The offer's open if you change your mind."

"Shall I fetch you around noon tomorrow and we'll go and visit the office of the building company?" Ava asked.

"Noon will be fine."

"I've got to help my mother at the markets in the morning, but I should be done by eleven."

* * *

When Ettie walked through the front door of her old house, she smelled something delicious cooking, and then she saw Elsa-May seated and glaring at her.

"Where have you been, Ettie? I've been waiting all day."

Ettie closed the front door and sat on the couch. "You haven't. You were at the knitting circle."

"You know what I mean. When I came home I expected you to be here. And who brought you home just now?"

"It was Ava Glick. We went to the police to see

what they were doing about Horace's murder. They seem to think Agatha did it."

Elsa-May raised her eyebrows. "They do?"

"*Jah.* We also visited Horace's *mudder* and *schweschder.* Sadie told the police about an argument that Horace and Agatha had. It's unlike Agatha to argue – she was so mild tempered."

"People can argue, but that doesn't cause them to kill."

Ettie nodded. "Now the police think that Horace and Agatha had some kind of lovers' tiff and she hit him over the head and killed him. Then they think she somehow managed to hide him under the floor."

"Do you think Sadie lied to the police?"

Ettie stared at Elsa-May and thought carefully about her answer. She didn't want to think of anyone as less than truthful. *"Nee,* I don't think she would lie."

"Maybe she believes what she said about the argument. That could be how she remembers things. It was a long time ago."

Ettie sighed. "I'm so tired. My mind's not working properly. Anyway, I'm going to stay at Agatha's *haus* tomorrow night."

"Do you want me to come with you?"

Ettie shook her head. *"Nee,* I'll go by myself."

"All right. It'll be strange to be here without you."

"I haven't been by myself for quite some time either." Once again, Ettie breathed in the aroma of something nice cooking. "You've got dinner on already?"

"Jah, I've got a pot roast with carrots, onions, potatoes, and turnips. Deidre gave us an apple pie."

"Goodie. I just realized how hungry I am."

"I watered the vegetables for you."

"You did?"

"I had to do something when I came home."

"Denke." Ettie leaned back in her couch and considered how much easier it was to live with another person. Elsa-May and she always shared the chores, and if she moved into Agatha's house she'd have to do everything herself.

71

Chapter 8

It was Thursday when Ava and Ettie took a taxi to the building company on the other side of town.

"How are we going to ask them about Horace, Ettie?"

"I haven't thought things through."

"I'm too nervous to say anything," Ava said.

"Best you keep quiet and let me do the talking," Ettie said. "I think an older woman will seem less threatening if anything happened back then."

Ava nodded.

The company office looked more like a lumberyard. The taxi pulled up outside eight-foot high wire fences topped with barbed wire.

"Here you are, ladies. Do you want me to wait for you?" the driver asked.

"No – we don't know how long we'll be." Ettie paid the driver, wondering if she should've asked him to wait. When she looked through the open gates she could see some kind of trailer home, which had the word 'office' printed on it in large block letters.

There was a worker on a forklift at one end and someone with a notebook in his hand walking away from them at the other. They were the only people visible as Ettie and Ava made their way to the office. Once they walked around the side of the makeshift building, they saw the office door was open. Ettie peered in. "Hello?"

"Yes," came a gruff male voice.

Ettie stepped in and saw a man who looked to be in his late thirties. "Hello, are you the boss?" The way the plump man was seated behind the desk told her that he was.

He looked Ettie up and down, then stood and extended his hand. "Yes, I'm Bill Settler."

"Ettie Smith, and this is my friend, Ava Glick."

He smiled at them as they made their way through the door.

"How can I help you?" he asked.

"We were wondering if we could take a few minutes of your time to ask you about someone who worked here many years ago."

"A few minutes? I can spare a few minutes." He smiled nicely and gestured toward some chairs. "Please, take a seat."

When they were both seated, Ettie began. "Many years ago – I'd say it would be before your time – a man by the name of Horace Hostetler worked here."

The man nodded. "I saw the piece in the paper. Someone said he once worked here. Sorry about what happened to him – was he a relative of yours?"

"A good friend."

"How can I help you?"

Ettie's mind went blank. Why was she there? She opened her mouth to speak hoping her brain would kick into gear.

"Who are you?"

The shrill voice belonged to an old woman. Ettie turned around to see an elderly lady at the door of the office.

"Oh no," Bill muttered to himself. "Excuse me for just one moment." He walked the elderly lady away, but not far enough. Ettie and Ava could hear their conversation.

"Ma, you drove here? You know the doctor told you not to drive."

"Forget that. Who's that in your office?" The woman sounded so cranky that Ettie and Ava raised their eyebrows at each other.

"It's no one, Ma. No one."

"Billy, you promised me you'd have no more to do with that woman."

"There are two women in my office and I don't know either of them. They're strangers; I've never met them before. They're after donations for charity. I'm writing out a check and then they'll leave. Now, you go home and I'll come and see you after work."

"You're sure you don't know them? Not lying to me again, are you?"

"No, ma, I'm telling you the God's honest truth."

"I've got some lunch for you and Chad in the backseat. Be a dear and fetch it?"

"We order lunch in. Just stop fussing. We're not

going to take the food."

Ettie stood and looked out the small window to see Bill put his hands on his hips.

He continued, "I'm going to have Tony drive you home, and he'll bring your car back here." The old lady didn't look too happy when Bill called one of his workers over to drive her home.

"But–"

"No. No more. I'll come over when I finish work today. Will that make you happy?"

"Make sure you do," Bill's mother said.

Once Bill was back with Ettie and Ava, he said, "Sorry about the interruption."

"Was that your mother?" Ettie asked.

Bill smiled and sat down. "Since my father died she's been – I don't know what the word is – overprotective, perhaps?"

Ettie laughed. "We never see our children as grown up. They'll always be little ones in our eyes."

"I suppose you're right." The corners of Bill's eyes creased as he smiled. "I'm not much better.

My boy wanted to leave school early and I insisted he work with me for a year before he goes anywhere else. He just seemed too young to be out in the big world."

"If you don't mind me saying, Mr. Settler, I overheard what your mother said. Do you know some people in our community?"

"We've had many Amish people work here, mostly when they're on their *rumspringa*. My mother's losing her mind and doesn't know what she's saying half the time." Bill laughed.

Ava put their conversation back on track. "We're here because we want to know if anyone who worked here might have known Horace Hostetler."

"I'm certain they would've, but I wouldn't know who knew him or who didn't. As you said, it was many years before my time. We've always had workers come and go." He raised his eyebrows slightly. "But you're in luck."

Ettie's face lit up and she leaned forward to hear why they were in luck regarding news of Horace's employment while he was on *rumspringa*.

Bill continued, "I've got records from back then down in one of the storage units. My father never threw anything away, and I'm afraid I've taken after him in that regard. Now we've got our records computerized, but I haven't been able to find it in me to throw the old paperwork out."

"Would you mind if we went through it?" Ava asked.

"It might take me days to find the exact year you're looking for."

Ettie told him the approximate years Horace would've worked there.

He looked at each of them in turn. "Can I ask you ladies what's so important?"

Ava and Ettie looked at each other.

"Are you trying to find out about his murder?" he asked before either lady could respond.

Ettie nodded. She didn't want to give too much away, but she had to say something to get the man to look for the information.

Bill leaned back in his chair. "You're trying to find who killed him and you think the man who killed him might have worked here? Is that it?"

Ava jumped in. "No, we just want to ask questions of people who knew him back then when he had left the community."

"Aren't the police doing that?" Bill asked.

"They have their own theories," Ettie said.

"The police haven't been by. Do you think they'll come around here asking questions?"

Ettie shrugged "I'm not sure."

"I'll help you all I can. I'll go through the records this afternoon. So you want a list of names of people who worked here at the same time as the man who was murdered?"

"Yes, Horace Hostetler."

The man grabbed a piece of paper out of the printer behind him and clicked on the end of his pen. He pushed the paper and pen toward Ettie. "You'd better write that name down for me."

Ettie wrote Horace's name and handed the paper back to Bill.

"Give me a couple days, and I'll have some names for you."

Ettie frowned. At first he said he'd look into it that afternoon and now he was saying two days? He didn't seem to be aware of the urgency. "Is there any way we can get those names sooner? We don't mind going through some old boxes or wherever you've got the papers stored."

Bill raised his brows. "That important, is it?"

Ettie and Ava nodded.

"I'll have my son, Chad, take you over to the storage shed where the records are kept. They've got the years on the end of the boxes. Now, as well as employee records there are sales receipts, taxation records – I'd ask you not to disturb anything."

"Thank you so much. You've been very helpful," Ettie said.

The man chuckled. "Well, you can put a good word in for me with the old guy upstairs."

Ava and Ettie smiled at him.

Bill walked past them and opened the door. Ettie could see a man standing not too far away and she wondered if he had been listening in.

"There you are, Chad – you were supposed to be

on the forklift today."

"Just taking a break, Pa."

"These ladies here need to be escorted over to the unit where we keep the old files. They're looking for people who worked here 'round the time of that guy they found under that house – the one that was in the paper."

Chad nodded. "Okay."

Bill pushed the door open for the ladies to walk out. "This is my son, Chad."

The ladies said hello.

Bill said, "Follow him, and please don't make a mess of the records. My father was meticulous, so please, leave everything where you find it."

Ava asked, "Might we borrow pen and paper to write with?"

"Of course you can." Bill went back into his office and came out with an empty notebook and two pens.

"Thank you, Mr. Settler. You've been so helpful."

He laughed. "I've been called many things in my time, but helpful – not so often." He looked at his son. "What are you waiting for?"

"This way," Chad said to the ladies.

Chapter 9

Ettie's eyes fell on the right box immediately – the years were written in large black letters on the end. She pointed at the box, knowing Horace had worked there in the mid-seventies. "There."

Chad pulled the box out for them. He leafed through the files until he found the ones with the employees. He handed some folders to Ettie.

Ettie leafed through them. "Here he is, Horace Hostetler. Write down these names, Ava." Ettie handed Ava a stack of papers. Each page contained an individual employee's name and address.

"That's going to take some time," Chad said. "Why don't you photocopy them?"

"Do you have a photocopier?" Ava asked.

"In my father's office, but he probably won't let you use it. You can take them with you and bring them back when you're done."

"Your father seemed protective of these records. I daren't take anything," Ettie said.

Chad shook his head. "We're only required to keep records for so many years – I think it's seven or something like that. We don't need to keep all these ancient ones." He flung his hand toward the rows of boxes. "I'll copy them for you, and I'll bring them by when I finish work."

Ettie looked at Ava. "What shall we do?"

Ava looked down at all pages in her hand. "Well, there's an awful lot here, Ettie."

"We've had a lot of people work here. People come and go all the time, always did. I don't mind doing it. Just tell me your address."

"It's on the other side of town."

"That's okay. I just got my license and I need the practice."

"That's awfully kind of you. Ava, why don't you write down our address for Chad?"

While Ava wrote, Chad asked, "What are you trying to find out?"

"The police think that Horace was killed by our friend who died recently. We know she didn't do it," Ettie said.

"You're trying to find out who really did kill him? Aren't you scared?"

"No, not a bit," Ettie admitted.

Chad's eyes widened. "You think one of these people killed him? Someone who used to work here?"

Ettie shook her head. "No, we just want to talk to someone he knew back then. You see, he left our Amish community briefly on what we call a *rumspringa* – that's when young people can leave our community for a time and they are free from following our rules. Anyway, we want to talk to people who knew him, people other than our Amish folk."

"I know, my father told me about the Amish. I hope you find something out. Why do the police think your friend did it, then? Surely they'd have to have some kind of evidence to suspect her."

"Someone told the police about an argument our friend had with him," Ava said.

Chad nodded. "I read about how the body was found under the floor of the house. Funny that the body was there for so long without anyone knowing. You'd think that a body would smell after a while. It would rot or something, wouldn't it?"

"He was wrapped up," Ava said. "In plastic."

"That's awful. I'd hate to have that job – the job of unwrapping the body. Who had to do that?"

Ettie pushed out her lips. "I don't know. I stayed inside when they were doing that."

"You were there?" Chad asked.

"Oh yes. It's my house." Ettie realized the boy didn't know the full story. "My friend left me the house, and my sister noticed something wrong with the floorboards so she had her grandson come take a look. He's a builder – my sister's grandson, my great nephew."

"Go on," Chad urged, his eyes wider still.

Ettie continued, "He lifted up a board, then went under the house and he found the body directly under the boards – the ones that weren't right."

"And did he – your sister's grandson – unwrap the body?"

"No, that's when we called the police."

"I read in the paper he was covered in plastic, but I thought he'd still stink. And wouldn't someone have looked for what was causing the smell? If I wrapped a dead animal in plastic, I'd reckon it would stink after some time."

"I don't know anything about that. I didn't know my friend very well back then," Ettie said.

Chad pushed his dark hair away from his face. "What did they find with him?"

Ettie frowned. "Like what?"

Chad shrugged his shoulders. "I don't know. I just think it's odd that he was under the house like that. The paper said he had no identification on him, nothing."

"That's right. Well, we better go now. Thank you for being so helpful," Ava said, handing him their address.

"I'll have these to you later on."

"Thank you, Chad. Where might we go to call for a taxi?" Ava asked.

He pulled a cell out of his pocket. "I'll call one

for you."

"We'll wait outside." Ava put her arm through Ettie's.

When they were out of the front gates, Ava said, "What a strange young man."

Ettie had to agree. "What do you make of him asking all those questions?"

"I don't know, but I didn't like it."

"I think he might be right about the body having an odor even though it was wrapped in plastic. I wonder why Agatha was never bothered by the smell?"

"Maybe she just didn't know what it was," Ava suggested. "Do you think that might be partly the reason the police think she did it?"

"Possibly. I know she wasn't the kind of woman not to look into something like a strange smell."

"Shall I see what I can find out? I know someone who works at a funeral home. I could ask him some questions and find out what would be expected in a situation like Horace's."

"*Jah,* do that," Ettie said.

"Okay. Do you think that young man asked too many questions?" Ava asked.

"Murder doesn't happen often around these parts. You know what people are like; he was probably just curious with it being in the newspaper and all."

Chapter 10

Ettie was alone in Agatha's house when Chad knocked on the door to deliver the photocopies as he'd said he would. When Ettie opened the door she was pleased to see him.

"There you go." He handed the pages to Ettie.

"Thank you. It was so kind of you to do this for us."

"No problem." He pinched the front of his loose white shirt and shook it. "It's so hot. Do you think I could have a glass of water?"

"Yes, come in."

Ettie headed to the kitchen with Chad close behind her. She placed the papers down on the kitchen table and proceeded to the sink. "I'm sorry I can't offer you chilled water." She turned away from the sink and was surprised to see him right behind her.

"This is fine," he said taking the glass from her. He drank quickly and handed her the empty glass.

"Thank you. I hope you find what you're looking for. I'll leave you to it." He turned and walked toward the front door with Ettie close behind. When he was in the middle of the living room, he stopped. "Where exactly did they find him?" His gaze swept across the floor.

Ettie thought it macabre that he would want to know, but like she'd said to Ava, he was probably just curious. "Around this area," Ettie said with a sweep of her hand. She had moved the rocking chair to the side of the room.

The boy pulled a face then looked up at Ettie. "A terrible way to go."

Ettie nodded, then walked past him to the front door, hoping he would follow. She opened the door and he walked out. "Thank you once again, Chad."

"Bye, Mrs. Smith."

Once he was gone, Ettie wasted no time in flicking through the stack of papers. Something about Chad struck her as odd. What if he'd left some names out? But why would he do that? Now Ettie regretted taking up his offer of delivering the copies to her home. He'd acted strangely and she was certain that she couldn't trust him.

Before long, Ettie heard Ava calling to her from the back door.

"Door's open, Ava."

Ava joined Ettie at the kitchen table. "I see Chad's been here?"

Ettie looked up from the pages. "Yes, and he asked where the body was found."

Ava shivered. "Weird."

"Anyway, did you speak to your friend from the funeral home?"

"Jah. Myles said that the body would still smell even though it was wrapped in plastic. He told me about a murder victim last year. The people living in an apartment block complained of a dreadful smell coming from one of the apartments. That's how the authorities were notified – because of the smell. And that body had been wrapped in layers of plastic."

"So the smell would've been bad. Well, there are no close neighbors here, and back then it was just

Agatha living in the house by herself with no one living in your *grossdaddi haus.*"

* * *

Elsa-May and Ettie arrived at the cemetery for the funeral of Horace Hostetler. The bishop was getting ready to give the message at the graveside when Ettie saw two cars amongst the buggies. She had to find out who the *Englischers* were.

"Ettie, are you looking at the cars?"

Ettie turned around and saw Ava, who continued, "Do you think that they might be some friends he had from all those years ago when he was on *rumspringa?*"

"How would they know about his funeral?"

"It was in the local paper. I've got a copy of it in my buggy. There's another article that came out in the paper this morning along with a picture of Horace as a young man – must've been taken when he was on *rumspringa.* It gives the whole story and gives the address of your *haus.*"

Knowing the Amish didn't read the *Englisch* papers, Ettie asked. "How did you know it was in there?"

"I didn't. Myles, my friend from the funeral home, told me. He came early this morning and asked if I wanted him to come with me today. I said no, but he did give me a copy of the paper if you want to see it."

"I'll have a look at it later," Ettie said. The outsiders were never hard to spot amongst the Amish. Ettie's gaze swept over the crowd. "Ava, there are two *Englisch* men standing over there. Why don't you go talk to them?"

"Why me?"

"Because I want to have another talk with Sadie."

Ava looked around as though she were looking for Sadie. "Here?"

"*Jah,* now go. We've no time to waste."

While Ava went off in the direction of the *Englischers,* Ettie caught sight of Sadie. Ettie walked toward her then stood close to her until she caught her eye.

"Hello, Ettie."

"Hello, Sadie. I see your cousins from Ohio are here?"

"Jah, the whole *familye* have come."

Ettie nodded. The look of sadness in Sadie's eyes deterred Ettie from asking her anything regarding Horace or Agatha.

Ettie was all too familiar with loss. She'd lost her parents, then her husband years ago, and two weeks ago she lost her constant canine companion; her loving dog, Ginger. Ettie rubbed Sadie's arm in an affectionate manner and Sadie smiled sweetly. Her talk with Sadie could wait for another day. Today was her time to say goodbye to the man she'd grown up with as her brother. There were other people heading over to talk to Sadie, so Ettie walked on and stood to the side where she'd get a good view of the people attending the funeral.

Ava appeared deeply involved in a conversation with the two men who looked like they knew each other. Could they be two men that Horace had worked with at the building company? Even though Horace would've known many more people when he was living as an *Englischer,* the building company was the only place they knew that he had worked.

When Ava came back, Ettie asked, "What did you find out?"

"One's a reporter and the other is an off-duty policeman."

Ettie was disappointed that they weren't people who knew Horace.

The bishop stood by Horace's grave plot, and then coughed loudly to draw everyone's attention. Four Amish men carried the coffin to the graveside. Ettie admired how fine they looked in their black suits and hats. They rested the coffin by the freshly dug grave while the bishop gave a lengthy talk about the meaning of this life and the life hereafter. Ettie stood next to Elsa-May, and while Ettie was being careful to appear as though she was listening to what the bishop had to say, she studied everyone in the crowd. She knew most of the Amish folk with the exception of Horace's Ohio relations.

Ettie's attention was drawn to a car that had just parked nearby. She strained her eyes to see who was getting out of the car. It was a man dressed in a dark suit and when he leaned against his car, Ettie was certain it was Bill Settler.

Elsa-May followed her sister's gaze. "Who's that?" she whispered.

"It's Bill Settler from the building company where Horace once worked. He's Horace's old boss' son."

"Hmm. It's awfully nice of him to pay his respects."

Ettie nodded and wondered why Bill stayed a distance away, and on further thought wondered why he'd come at all.

Chapter 11

O nce the funeral was over, Elsa-May asked, "Are you coming home tonight, Ettie, or staying at the new *haus?*"

"I'll stay at Agatha's *haus*. Ava's a little worried about being on her own. She feels safer with me there."

"Very well. Jeremiah's driving me home. Are you going home with Ava or shall I have Jeremiah take you?"

"I'll go with Ava, *denke.*" Ettie looked around to see if Mr. Settler was still there, but his car had gone. Turning back to see Elsa-May walking away, Ettie called after her, "I'll come by tomorrow."

"Are you ready to go?" Ava asked.

"Oh, there you are, Ava. Did you see Bill Settler standing by his car?"

"Nee. Where was he?"

"He parked his car just behind that white one. He watched from a distance for a few moments before he disappeared."

"Are you sure it was him?"

"Pretty certain. *Jah.* As certain as I am that I'm looking at you right now."

Ava walked toward her buggy and Ettie walked alongside. "I've been thinking about a few things, Ettie. How was the body wrapped exactly? Was it only in plastic? They said they couldn't get any DNA material from the skeleton or something of that nature. So does that mean he was only a skeleton?"

"I took it that they meant they wouldn't have any DNA material from the killer because he had rotted away so much."

"How could we find out?" Ava asked.

Ettie chuckled. "I'm not going back near Detective Kelly anytime soon."

"Would Jeremiah know?" Ava asked. "I'm mean, since he was there at the time?"

Ettie drew her eyebrows together while she thought. "Elsa-May was outside when the police came. She didn't talk about it, though. I wonder if she knows more about the body. I'll ask her when I go home tomorrow. I'm going to Agatha's tonight and tomorrow I'll visit Elsa-May."

"It must be confusing. I guess you'll have to pick a place soon, where you want to live."

"All in good time. I've come to learn that when you give things time, the right decisions become obvious. I used to make quick decisions when I was younger – I was always in such a rush – but now that I'm older and moving more slowly, I realize that things always have a way of sorting themselves out."

"I guess that makes sense. If you live a little bit in both places, you'll soon know where you're happiest."

"Something like that, dear, something like that."

Ava dropped Ettie by her front door and then continued on to the barn to tend to her horse.

Ettie pushed her front door open, and she didn't go more than two steps when she saw something was wrong. She gasped and walked two more steps. The whole living room had been destroyed. Every floorboard had been taken up. She walked farther and looked down at the dirt below the house. Only the cross joists remained.

She hurried out the door to fetch Ava. "Ava, come quick."

"What is it?" Ava said as she jumped down from the buggy she'd just stopped near the barn.

Between gasps, Ettie said, "All the boards in the main room have been taken up. Go call the police. Try to speak to Detective Kelly; tell him it's urgent."

"The floorboards?"

"*Jah,* Ava, hurry – go now."

While Ava raced to the end of the road to call the police, Ettie sat on the front steps of her new home. It was an uncanny feeling, knowing that someone had entered uninvited and violated what had been a peaceful home for her friend of many years. She looked down the road to the nearest neighbor, now grateful that she and Elsa-May had people living close on either side. If there had been people living closer to here, they would've been sure to hear some noise. But Agatha had liked her large parcel of land, which allowed her to keep a few animals and have a large barn.

If Elsa-May hadn't gotten those new glasses and seen the marks on the floor, they might never have known that Horace was under the house. Pulling herself to her feet, Ettie decided to walk around the house to see what she could see. The disruption that had come to the house since it had been given to her made her wonder if she should continue to live with Elsa-May. It was nice to have family around in emergencies.

"Are you all right?"

Ettie looked over to see that Ava had returned.

"Jah, I'm okay. Did you talk to the detective?"

Ava nodded. "They're coming soon. Wait in my place while I put the horse and buggy away."

Ettie walked into Ava's *grossdaddi haus* and put the pot on the stove. A cup of tea always made her feel better. When she sat at the table, Ava came through the door. "Ava, I know you said you talked to the detective, but did you speak to Detective

105

Kelly directly?"

Ava shook her head and slumped into a chair. "Nee, but I told them my message the other day was not passed on. I insisted they tell him, and they said they would. They told me someone would come out straight away."

"Tea?" Ettie asked.

"Jah, that would be nice."

Ettie and Ava sat drinking tea while they waited for the police.

"They take a long time." Ettie looked up at that moment, and heard a car pulling up outside. "Ah, that must be them. Let's go."

Ettie was pleased to see Detective Kelly. At last he was taking things seriously. She showed the detective and the two officers with him the destruction to her house.

"What do you think, Detective?" Ettie asked.

The detective got as close as he could and looked at the damage. "I'd say it was some crazed souvenir hunter. We've had them before; very often they try to find something to auction online." He looked back to Ava and Ettie. "They wouldn't have found anything. I had my men comb the area the day after we found the body."

"They didn't find anything?" Ava asked.

"No."

"Shouldn't you take fingerprints or something?" Ettie asked.

The detective looked at Ettie and then walked toward the front door. He leaned down and said, "No sign of forced entry." He directed the two officers to walk around the house and find the point of entry.

"I didn't lock the door," Ettie said.

The detective's mouth fell open. "Why not?"

Ettie pulled a face. "I never do when I go out during the day. No one locks their doors around here." When Ettie saw the detective looking at her in disbelief she added, "I lock it at night when I go to sleep."

Detective Kelly shook his head. "I know you trust your neighbors and you're surrounded by your Amish people, but anyone can come into the area."

Ava said, "They could've just as easily come up through the floorboards, couldn't they? If they were looking for something under the house?"

The detective ignored Ava, kept looking at Ettie, and took a deep breath. "I suggest you find yourself somewhere else to stay tonight."

"Stay with me, Ettie." Ava placed a hand on Ettie's shoulder.

"I might as well since I'm here already. Will you have the fingerprint team go over the place for evidence?" Ettie looked up at the detective who towered above her.

He shook his head. "Trespassing and damage to property are crimes, but Mrs. Smith, you left your front door open."

"Unlocked, Detective. The door was closed."

Kelly heaved a sigh. "I'll see what the men have found and I'll make a report." He looked back over his shoulder at the loose boards that had been thrown in a corner. "Do you have someone to fix this?"

"I've got my great nephew, Jeremiah. He's a builder."

"He's the one who found Horace," Ava said.

"Ah, yes. I met him the other night. Well, very good." He looked at Ava. "And you'll look after Mrs. Smith tonight?"

Ava nodded. "I will. She'll be fine with me."

The detective walked out the door.

Ava put her arm around Ettie's shoulder. "It's nearly dinnertime. I'll heat us up some soup."

"Tomorrow morning do you think you could tell Jeremiah what happened and have him come as soon as he can? I don't like to leave it like this for too long."

"Jah, I will. Don't worry about another thing. You can sleep in my bed tonight and I'll take the sofa."

"Nee, I can't put you out like that."

"I won't hear another word, Ettie – you're taking the bed."

Ettie smiled and nodded, then tried to remember if she'd told Elsa-May she'd be back that night, or whether she told her she'd be staying at Agatha's house.

Chapter 12

Ettie woke to hammering coming from the main house. When she saw how light it was she knew she'd slept in. The noise had to be Jeremiah already at work fixing her floor. She got up and looked around for her dress. Ava had been good enough to loan her a nightgown. She closed the bedroom door and saw her dress hanging on a clothes peg. After she changed into her dress and *kapp*, she looked around the *grossdaddi haus* for Ava. When she realized Ava wasn't in any of the rooms, she peered out the window and saw Ava's horse was gone, too.

Ettie went straightaway to see how Jeremiah was getting along with the work. She pushed her door open and saw Jeremiah leaning over, placing the boards back. He looked up when he saw her.

"Aunt Ettie, I found something." He placed his hammer down, stood, and stepping on the joists, made his way over to the side of the room. Ettie stepped forward to see what it was. Jeremiah picked something off the windowsill and made his way over to hand it to her. "There's a key inside." Jeremiah wiped his sweaty forehead with the sleeve of his shirt.

Ettie examined the small, rectangular envelope in her hand. It seemed brittle and she was almost afraid to handle it. It was undoubtedly old from the yellowing of the paper. The number 157 was printed on the outside.

"There's a key inside," Jeremiah said.

"Yes, I heard you, but I'm still looking at the envelope. From the look of it, it's been here for some time. Where exactly did you find it?"

"It was taped flat to one of the boards inside a strip of brown paper. At first I didn't see it because it was the same color as the wood."

Ettie opened the envelope and dropped the key into the palm of her hand. It was unlike any key she'd seen before. "I think the detective needs to see this."

"Does it open something around here, do you

think?" Jeremiah asked.

"Nee, Jeremiah. I would say most certainly it doesn't."

The sound of a buggy outside told Ettie that Ava was back. Ettie hurried out of the house to Ava, who had just pulled up outside the barn. When Ettie reached her she said, "Ava, *denke* for fetching Jeremiah this morning."

"That's fine, Ettie. I went early and stopped by the markets on my way home. Is something wrong?" Ava stepped down from the buggy.

"Ava, Jeremiah found something. He found a key. I'm sure that's what the people were looking for."

"The ones who ripped up the floor?"

Ettie nodded. "I'm certain that they were looking for this key." Ettie passed Ava the key and she turned it over and studied it carefully.

"Why weren't the police able to find it? They were under the house for some time looking for evidence."

"It was taped flat, Jeremiah said, hidden by

brown paper that matches the boards. They might not have been looking for things like that. They were most likely looking for things in the ground, or under the dirt."

Ava nodded.

"Can you drive me to show Detective Kelly?" Ettie asked.

"*Jah,* okay. Can I have breakfast first? I've brought us some fresh baked bread from the markets."

"*Wunderbaar,* and I'll see if your chickens have laid eggs."

"They aren't my chickens, Ettie."

"They aren't? Are they mine?"

Ava laughed. "I don't know, Agatha didn't say who she wanted to have the chickens."

"I'm too old to look after chickens, and I know enough people who give Elsa-May and me eggs all the time. You can have them if you want them."

Ava smiled. "*Jah,* I'd like them."

"That's one thing settled," Ettie said. "Hopefully by the end of the day we'll have a few more things settled around here."

* * *

"It's just a key, Mrs. Smith. I'm sure if you dig under any house in this county you'd find a key or two," Detective Kelly said. He barely looked at Ava or Ettie. By the way his mouth was clamped tight and his cheeks sucked in, Ettie knew that he was severely annoyed they'd come to see him. He hadn't asked them into his office, but with an armful of files clutched to his chest, spoke to them at the front desk in earshot of everyone nearby.

Ettie offered the yellowed envelope to the detective so he could inspect it and the key. "This doesn't look like just any key, and it was hidden, taped onto a board – underneath the floor. This might be what they'd come back to find."

The detective slammed down the folders he was holding onto the front desk. "Look, Mrs. Smith, we do like the support of the community, but you're crossing the line and bordering on being obstructive. You seem to think that we're doing nothing. I've had our evidence technicians comb the area and we've taken samples of dirt from under your house. The matter is heavily under investigation." He leaned his body forward and stuck out his lower jaw. "You're not being helpful, you're being a hindrance." He straightened up and tipped his head to the side and stared at Ettie. "Now, if you'll excuse me, I've got work to do."

Ettie pushed out her lips.

"C'mon, Ettie," Ava said tugging at her arm.

"Do you want to take it in as evidence, at least?" Ettie asked. "It's an unusual shaped key. Won't you just take a quick look at it?"

The detective rolled his eyes before saying, "I'm done."

Ettie and Ava stood there watching as the detective walked away. The two seated policemen staring at them from behind the front desk caught Ettie's attention.

Ettie stepped back and whispered to Ava, "It's time to do our own investigations."

Ava raised her eyebrows. "How?"

"That name the detective gave us the other day – Terence something."

"Terence Wheeler?"

"Jah, that was it. Why don't we start by looking up that name on the library computer? You can look up the Internet, can't you?"

"Jah, of course I can, but what about the key?"

"The key isn't going anywhere for the moment." Ettie stuck the envelope containing the key up her sleeve.

Ava nodded. "Let's go then. The library's only down the road."

"I've used the computer at the library before, but I'm sure you'll be faster and more capable."

Ava giggled. "Ettie, you're full of surprises."

* * *

Ava punched some things into one of the library computers and read what was on the screen. "Terence Wheeler was incarcerated numerous times for robberies. He specialized in jewelry and diamond theft."

"It pays to specialize, they say." Ettie peered over Ava's shoulder.

"He's dead," Ava announced suddenly.

"Really? What else does it say about him? When did he die?" Ettie sat down in the chair next to her.

"In 1975 he was arrested for the Tonkins jewelry heist, but charges were dropped. He was identified as being at the scene of the crime, but the jewelry was never recovered."

"That was around the same time Horace disappeared. Look up the Tonkins jewelry heist, see what you can find out," Ettie ordered.

"Okay, let's see now." Ava pressed the keys on the computer while Ettie leaned back in her chair. "The Tonkins were a wealthy couple visiting from England. They had jewelry and diamonds they'd just purchased in an auction. Until they left town they were kept in a safe at the hotel where they were staying. Just before they booked out, two of the hotel staff were taking the jewelry back to their suite when two men wearing black masks held them up at gunpoint. Some of the hotel staff recognized Wheeler as being in the hotel that morning."

"Hardly grounds for arrest, I would think," Ettie said.

"A huge coincidence, though. Why would he have been at the hotel when he had a home in the area?"

"He could've been visiting someone, or having a meal. Does it say anything else?"

Ava scrolled down the screen. "That's all it says. The jewelry was never recovered and they had to drop the charges against the man."

"I wonder if Crowley was around back then…"

"Your old detective friend?"

"That's the one. I think it's time to pay him a visit." Ettie wrote down a number for Ava. "Here, phone this number and tell Crowley that I'd like him to come to my place this afternoon. Give him my new address."

"Okay." Ava took the number from Ettie and headed to the public telephone in the foyer of the library.

Minutes later, Ava returned. "He'll be there at two."

"We best get back to the house."

* * *

Ava left Ettie to talk to Crowley alone. He'd been retired a while and she looked forward to seeing him again. She sat in the living room until she heard a car, then she opened the front door for him.

"New house, Ettie?" Crowley asked as he walked toward her.

"A good friend left me this house. It's a long story."

"Elsa-May's well, I hope?"

"She is." Ettie patted Crowley on his arm. "It's nice to see you again."

"Likewise."

"Well, come in." Ettie walked inside and when Crowley followed she closed the door after him.

"Come through to the living room."

When Crowley sat, he said, "It seems bigger than your old house, but it looks as though there are lots of repairs needed." He frowned as he looked around the room.

He was right; both the inside and the outside sorely needed painting, the gutters needed fixing and judging by the uneven floor, the footings – or at least some of them – needed attention.

"Your friend said you wanted to see me urgently?"

Ettie told Crowley everything about Horace and Agatha and then what had happened to her floor.

"Wheeler was a known criminal. He was often arrested but we weren't able to make any of the charges stick. I helped work on one of his arrests, but I'd only just joined the force, so I was only shuffling papers on the case. We were going after Wheeler and another criminal, Settler. They were adversaries. The two of them hated each other, that was well known."

Ettie handed him the small envelope. He tipped

the key into his hand.

"This is what my great nephew found when he was nailing my floorboards back. He's a builder, you see, and he's Elsa-May's grandson."

He held the key up. "This is a safe deposit box key."

"Good. And what's that?" Ettie asked.

"If someone wants to keep something safe, they can lease a box from the bank. Many people keep important paperwork or private things in their boxes."

"Jewelry?"

"Certainly. Coins, jewelry, gold, all those kinds of things." He turned the envelope over. "With any luck, the number on this envelope will correspond with the number of the box. They don't normally have the number on the key."

"You've seen these keys before?" Ettie asked.

Crowley nodded. "They're all usually square like this, with these flat grooved edges." He ran his finger along the key to show Ettie what he meant.

"I think the person who destroyed my house was

looking for this key."

"You mentioned Terence Wheeler before – what did Detective Kelly say about him?"

"He asked if we'd heard his name. We said no, and that's all that was said."

"We?" Crowley asked.

"Ava was with me. Ava lives in the *grossdaddi haus* attached to this place. It's like a small apartment. Anyway, Ava and I went to the library to look up Terence Wheeler and we found out that he might have been involved in a big robbery."

Crowley nodded. "Yes, the one involving the English couple who were robbed at their hotel."

"Do you think this might be Terence Wheeler's key? Maybe Horace knew something and was killed because of it."

"Did Horace know Terence Wheeler?"

"I don't know; Detective Kelly didn't say. All he said was that his name had come up in his investigations around Horace."

"You said the key was taped to one of the boards?"

Ettie nodded. "So it was unlikely that it was dropped – it was hidden deliberately."

"It seems so, Ettie."

"Why would Wheeler hide the key under my house?"

"He could've been coming back to get it. He died not long after his arrest, and from what you've said that corresponds with the time that Horace went missing."

"Do you think Wheeler killed Horace?"

Crowley shook his head. "From what you've told me so far, there's not enough evidence to say anything of the sort."

"Tell me more about these boxes. If someone loses the key can't they just go to the bank and say they've lost it? And the bank opens it for them?"

"It's not as easy as that. The person would need to sign a stack of paperwork; it would take about two weeks before the bank could arrange to have the box drilled open. Not the best way for someone to hide stolen jewelry."

"He's dead now, so no one will be getting into

his box, I guess. Not without the key."

"Sometimes a bank will shut down someone's box when they know someone's died. It's hard for relatives to get the contents out; there's a lot of red tape involved."

"How can one tell which bank the key belongs to?" Ettie asked.

"You can't. Detective Kelly would have to get a warrant and start with the local banks. Not all banks have safe deposit boxes. I'm certain only one in town does." Crowley looked down at the key. "I'm guessing it's too late to bother with prints?" He looked across at Ettie.

"I'm afraid so. I'm sorry, but we didn't realize the importance of it. We've both touched it, Ava and I, and so has Jeremiah."

Crowley slipped the key back inside the envelope before placing it in his inner coat pocket. "It'll be very interesting to find out who this key belongs to."

"I don't know if you'll have any luck speaking to that new detective," Ettie said.

Crowley scratched his neck. "Don't you worry about that, Ettie."

Crowley stood and disappeared out the door. Ettie was happy that someone was finally listening. Crowley had been a little like Detective Kelly when she first knew him.

Ettie had just sat down with a cup of tea when she heard a knock at the door. She knew it wasn't Ava because she always came to the back door. Maybe Crowley's forgotten something. When she flung the door open, there before her stood Sadie.

"Sadie, how nice to see you. Come in. Come through to the kitchen – I've just made a pot of tea."

"Denke, Ettie." Sadie followed Ettie into the kitchen, dragging her feet. When Sadie was seated, she began. "Oh, Ettie, I'm just so upset over everything that's happened. I'm too upset to live."

"Life has its low points, but don't go saying things like that. How's your *mudder* coping now?"

"Still upset. Your visit the other day cheered her up. I always thought he had died, and that's why he never came back." She balled her hand into a fist and held it against her stomach. "I felt he was dead." Sadie looked up at Ettie. "I didn't want it to be true."

Ettie racked her brain, trying to come up with words of comfort. "There, there, Sadie. He's at home with *Gott*, and he's happy now."

Sadie nodded. "Oh, Ettie, I hope you don't mind me coming here to talk to you. I don't have many close friends and if I talk to *mamm* I know she'll start crying all over again and not be able to stop."

"That's perfectly all right. Talk to me whenever you want. I remember how close you always were to Horace."

"You do?"

Ettie nodded.

"*Jah*, we were close, weren't we?'

"You were." Ettie desperately wanted to ask her questions but feared now was not the time to do so.

"There's another reason I came here today."

Ettie raised her eyebrows.

Sadie continued, "I was hoping that you might

have found something here in this house that belonged to Horace, since he was so close to Agatha. I'd like a memento, something to remember him by."

"Wouldn't he have left all his belongings at your *haus?* Surely all his possessions were left there."

"*Mamm* threw everything out a long time ago when he didn't come home. She thought he was living as an *Englischer* so she wanted to rid the place of his memory."

"I can sympathize with you, and your *mudder.* I've been through the pain of losing someone many a time." Ettie thought about her dog that had just died. No one or nothing would be able to replace him. "But, as Bishop John would say, death is a part of life."

"*Jah,* but why did he have to go so soon?"

"*Nee.* He was still very young, but none of us knows when our time will come."

As Sadie sipped her tea, Ettie noticed Sadie's red-rimmed eyes and her paler-than-usual skin. She remembered the pain of losing her own brother.

"There was a key found near him."

Sadie gulped on her tea, then wiped her mouth with her fingers. "A key? Where is it?"

"On its way to the police. They should have it by now," Ettie answered.

"Why the police?"

Ettie decided not to tell her about the floor being taken up. "Evidence I suppose, much like his clothing."

Sadie nodded. "Do you know what the key is for, what it unlocks?"

"Nee, I don't." She paused. "All that's happened shows us that we have to appreciate those we have, while we have them."

"That's true, Ettie."

A loud knock sounded on the door. Ettie opened it to see a young man dressed in black. "I don't want any trouble, lady, I just want the key."

"What key?"

The young man reached behind him and pulled a gun from his back pocket. "I want the key and I know you've got it."

"I did have a key, but I gave it to the police. A detective was here and took it to them."

Sadie stepped forward. "Put that gun down! It's true; she doesn't have it."

The man shifted his weight from one foot to the other. The gun shook when he said, "You better not be lying to me lady or I'll be back." He glanced over his shoulder with the gun still shaking in his hands. He looked back at Ettie and then ran away.

Ettie stepped outside and looked to see the young man get into the passenger-side door of a black car before it zoomed away.

Ettie put a hand to her heart to try and stop it from racing. "The way you spoke to him just now – Sadie, why weren't you scared of him?

Sadie sighed. "Sit down. It's a long story and I need to unburden my heart."

Sadie helped Ettie to a chair.

"Just before Horace disappeared, he told me a little of what was happening. Horace's boss was also running another business – against the law."

"Stealing things?"

"Jah."

"What was his boss' name?"

"Settler, Bertram Settler."

Ettie's eyes flew to the ceiling. *Bertram Settler would've been Bill Settler's father. Bill Settler, from the construction company.* "I didn't mean to interrupt you, Sadie. Continue; I'm listening."

"His rivals – well, Horace called them his boss' enemies – were Terence Wheeler's gang. I urged Horace to come back to the community; I knew no good would come of him knowing people like that."

"Go on."

"I heard from someone Horace knew that a man called Terence Wheeler said a key was hidden with Horace's body, but where no one would be able to find it. That's the first I heard that Horace was dead."

Ettie gasped and her mouth fell open. "Who told you about all of that? And do you know what the key opens?"

Sadie hung her head.

"Do you know who sent that man?" Ettie persisted but still Sadie made no reply.

Ettie frowned, pushing her lips together. "Who was that young man and why did he listen to you?"

Sadie shrugged. "He didn't listen to me."

"It certainly seemed that way. Look, Sadie, if you know anything, anything at all – and it appears that you do – it's best you talk about it. If you don't want to tell me, tell the police, but someone needs to know."

Sadie stared at Ettie with large, round eyes.

Ettie continued, her voice louder. "That man just now, or whoever sent him, must want whatever that key opens, and judging by the gun, they might be prepared to kill for it. I don't know about you, but I'd rather die of old age since the Lord's spared me for this long."

"Do you think someone else might get killed?"

Ettie nodded. "We need to tell the police about this. And you need to tell them everything you know – do it now."

Sadie stood. "You're right, Ettie, of course,

you're right. I'll go and see them right away."

Ettie took a deep breath and put her hand on her heart. *"Jah*, okay. I'll sit here and try to recover. If they want to talk to me they can come here, or I'll go into the station tomorrow. I can't do any more today."

After Sadie left, Ettie had a lie down on the bed in Agatha's spare room, trying to get images of the gun out of her head.

It was just before dinnertime when Ava knocked on Ettie's back door. Ettie couldn't sleep and was glad for the interruption. She ushered her in and told her everything that had happened with Sadie and the man with the gun.

"Ettie, you poor thing! Let me cook you dinner."

"That would be *gut, denke*. I feel so much better now that Crowley's involved. He's taking the key to Kelly and hopefully he'll get a search warrant for the box at the bank."

"How would the man know you had the key?" Ava asked.

Ettie said, "There were only four of us who

knew. You, me, Jeremiah, and Crowley – but then again, Detective Kelly did have us talking at the front of the police station."

"That's true, and you said you found the key stuck to the boards. Anyone could have overheard it."

"There were the two officers behind the desk, and people coming and going. I don't remember anyone in particular that seemed to be listening. Sadie knew of the existence of a key, she'd heard those rumors regarding Terence Wheeler, a key and Horace's body. I wonder why she never told the police that before now."

Chapter 13

Ettie again spent the night with Ava in the *grossdaddi haus*. The next morning, Ava had left early to help her mother with some work at the farmers market. When Ettie heard a knock on the door, she looked out the window to see Crowley.

"Come in," she said as she opened the door.

"Oh, good, you're here. The young lady who lives here told me where you were."

"I stayed here last night after everything that happened." Ettie stepped back to allow Crowley to step through.

As he walked in, he said, "I've got some good news. Kelly finally agreed to get a warrant. Mind you, I was with him most of the day trying to persuade him, and then he had me helping him go over all the evidence."

"Good. Have a seat." Crowley and Ettie sat at the small kitchen table. "Then you would've been there when Sadie told Kelly all about the man with the gun?"

Crowley frowned. "About what?"

"I thought you would've heard."

"No, I've heard nothing. There was a man with a gun?"

"Sadie came here yesterday, and while she was here a man came and pointed a gun at me. He demanded the key. Somehow he'd heard that I had it."

"Ettie, you should have called the police straight away."

"Sadie said she was going to go straight to the police station when she left here."

"Well, she didn't. I was with Kelly most of the day and no mention was made of it." Crowley sprang to his feet and whipped his cell out of his pocket. "I need to make a call." Crowley strode outside.

Ettie hadn't had a chance to tell him the rest of her news.

Crowley came back. "There was no report made by her at all." Crowley rubbed his furrowed brow.

"Is there some mistake? Perhaps she called instead of going there in person."

Crowley shook his head and placed his hands on his hips. "Tell me exactly what happened."

"I haven't told you everything. Sit down." When Crowley sat, Ettie said, "The man said he knew I had the key and Sadie stepped forward and said that I didn't. He believed her and not me. I thought that odd."

Ettie saw by the detective's face he didn't think that it was particularly odd.

"And, what's more, she might have been hinting for the key, too, before the man got there. She asked if Horace had left anything at Agatha's, saying she wanted something to remember him by. Then after the man with the gun ran away, she told me that someone told her that a man called Terence Wheeler said that he'd hidden a key with Horace's body. She wouldn't tell me who told her that."

Crowley groaned. "Kelly's sending someone to talk to her now, then we'll know more. Do you believe what she told you, Ettie?"

Ettie blinked rapidly. "I have no reason to believe otherwise." Ettie pulled her mouth to one side. "I wonder why she didn't go to the police when she said she would. What about the young man who pointed a gun at me?"

Crowley nodded. "I'm sure that Kelly will want you to have a look at some mug shots."

Ettie pulled a face, but when Crowley remained quiet, Ettie nodded. "I will if I have to, but I wouldn't recognize him again. He just looked like any other young man, and all I was looking at was the gun."

"Why don't you go back home with Elsa-May until all this is over with? It's too much for you to stay here with everything that's happened."

Ettie wondered if that might be best. She did miss Elsa-May – even though she was dominating and overbearing at times, it was nice to have her company.

"Come on. I'll take you there now."

"Thank you. I'll leave a note for Ava. She might be scared on her own too, but I'll let her know to she can stay with me if she gets frightened."

"Okay. There's no rush; I'll wait in the car. I've got some calls to make."

Crowley drove Ettie back to the home she shared with Elsa-May. She hoped Elsa-May had been watering her plants, and wouldn't be too cross with her for not being there.

When he stopped the car in front of the house, Ettie said, "Do come in; Elsa-May has most likely just baked something."

Crowley smiled. "I've missed her cooking, and yours too, Ettie. It wouldn't hurt to have a small sample."

Ettie laughed. "We'll fatten you up yet."

He followed Ettie into the house.

"Elsa-May, I've got Detective Crowley with me."

Elsa-May came out of the kitchen smiling. "It's good to see you again. Have you come to help us find out who killed Horace? I told Ettie to let you have your retirement in peace."

Ettie frowned at Elsa-May. She was the one

who'd said to let him have his retirement in peace. She didn't want to argue in front of Crowley, but she'd certainly give Elsa-May a piece of her mind when he left. "He's helping us and that's that."

"I don't mind. The first few months of peace and quiet were good, but then the days wear on and they're pretty much the same."

"You're okay with helping, then?" Ettie asked.

"I'm pleased to be back in the swing of things."

"I'll put the pot on the stove, then, and see if I can find some cake." Elsa-May hurried back to the kitchen.

After Crowley sat down, Ettie said, "See, I told you there'd be cake."

Before long, they were all seated with tea and fresh orange cake while Ettie told Elsa-May all the events she'd missed.

The sound of Crowley's loud ring tone from his cell caused Ettie to jump.

He sprang to his feet. "Excuse me, I'll take this outside."

When Crowley was gone, Elsa-May said,

"You're awfully jumpy, Ettie."

"A lot's happened. I had a gun pointed at me."

"Jah, you told me. That can't have been good."

Crowley walked back through the door. "It appears that Sadie Hostetler never came home last night. She's disappeared."

Ettie's jaw fell open and her hand flew to her mouth. "Do you think she's in danger?"

"We can't be too careful, but you did say that the man put the gun down when she told him to. I think we can safely assume that she's involved in some way with this whole debacle."

"It wasn't like that. She told that young man I didn't have the key, then after that he left." Ettie nibbled the end of her fingernail.

"Young man?" Elsa-May asked Ettie.

"The one who pointed the gun at me." Ettie shook her head at Elsa-May – hadn't she been listening?

The two ladies looked back up at Crowley and he sat down.

"Looks like there's a whole lot more to this than first appeared," he said.

"I'm sorry to drag you into all this now that you've retired," Ettie said.

Elsa-May jutted out her bottom jaw. "That's what I said in the first place. Leave him be; he's retired."

Ettie rolled her eyes.

"Anytime you need me, I'm always there," Crowley said with a smile tugging the corners of his lips. He reached for his teacup.

"Yes, you've been good to us in the past." Elsa-May glanced over at Ettie who narrowed her eyes at her.

"I wonder where Sadie could've gone to," Ettie said.

Elsa-May said, "Would her mother know?"

"I don't know. I don't think she'd want her mother involved. Doris is too old to cope with the worry, which is why I'm surprised that Sadie's disappeared." Ettie turned to Crowley. "Do you think she's in danger? Maybe that man with the gun didn't leave and he was lurking up the road."

"Let's not think about that for now. The police

are doing everything they can."

"Poor Sadie. Things never seem to go her way. She was jilted by two men before she was twenty."

Elsa-May's eyebrows raised. "Ettie, stop it. You like to gossip far too much. That's how rumors start. Rumors are spread by people with too much time on their hands and not enough sense in their heads. Anyway, I heard she was only jilted by one man."

The lines in Crowley's forehead deepened. "Ettie, you said Sadie seemed to be familiar with the man who had the gun, and didn't seem afraid?"

"She wasn't scared at all. He insisted I had the key and then she came next to me and said the police had it."

"When she stood next to you, did he point the gun at her?"

Ettie shook her head.

Crowley took a notepad out of his pocket and made some notes.

Ettie licked her lips. "I don't know what to think anymore."

"Would it be possible she knew the man?" Crowley asked.

"No, I don't think she knew him when I think about it now. But that's what my first thought was. Anyone else could have overheard us at the station when I was talking to Kelly and trying to have him take a look at it."

"Hmm," Crowley said. "This does put another slant on things." He stretched out his arm and took another piece of orange cake.

"What do we do know so far?" Elsa-May leaned forward in her chair.

When Crowley swallowed his mouthful of cake, he said, "Leave it to Kelly. He's getting a search warrant for the deposit box – we're taking a guess that it's the local bank, since there's only one in town with box facilities."

"How long will it take them to get a warrant?" Elsa-May asked.

"He'll have to gather enough evidence to prove to the judge that there are grounds to sign off on a warrant."

"Someone's dead – wouldn't that be grounds enough?" Elsa-May asked.

"It's a key, but it might not be related to this whole thing. The judge will have to be convinced that this key is related to Horace's murder. It will help him get the warrant now that someone with a gun was after it." He looked at Ettie. "I think you'll have to make another visit to Kelly."

"I'll go tomorrow," Ettie said, not looking forward to doing so.

* * *

The next morning, Ettie was feeling guilty about leaving Ava alone in the *grossdaddi haus* after all that had happened. She made Ava the first stop of the day before she went to visit old Mrs. Hostetler.

When she got out of the taxi, she saw that Jeremiah was working inside her house. She stepped through the door. "Jeremiah? I thought you'd finished."

"Hiya, Aunt Ettie. I should have this done by

lunchtime. I'm just going over the nails, making sure they're safe and filling the cracks. I had another job to get to yesterday so I couldn't finish this. I'm going to give it a light polish when I'm done. It'll look great."

"It's looking good already. *Denke,* Jeremiah." Ettie heard from the sound of the hoof beats passing the house that Ava was pulling up in the buggy. She went out to meet her. "Where have you been so early?" Ettie asked.

"I'm coming home. I stayed at *Mamm's* last night. I was a little scared to stay here alone."

"You got my note?"

"I did, and I didn't want to intrude. *Mamm* was happy for my company."

Ettie walked beside Ava's buggy up to the stable. "You'll never guess what's happened."

"What?"

Ettie told Ava everything that had happened in her absence, and then added,

"Sadie's disappeared. The last thing she told me was she was going to the police and she didn't.

146

When they went to her home to question her, they found she'd disappeared."

"Oh, Ettie. Do you think she's frightened? Or maybe the killer's got her?"

Ettie shrugged her shoulders. "Don't know. I'm on my way now to see old Mrs. Hostetler to ask if she knows where Sadie is. Detective Crowley said I should go and make a report about the man with the gun who was after the key, but I'll do that later."

"Well, I best take you both places."

Ettie smiled. "I was hoping you would."

* * *

Ava and Ettie's first stop was Doris Hostetler.

"Ettie, and Ava, I wish I could tell you both. It would be such a burden lifted from my shoulders. I made a promise to certain people that I wouldn't breathe a word of what they told me." Mrs. Hostetler said.

Ettie could feel Ava's eyes on her; they both

knew it was a long shot that Sadie's mother would tell them anything. "Who did you promise?" Ettie asked.

Mrs. Hostetler shook her head. "I can say no more. I've already said too much."

"Did you tell the police anything?" Ettie asked.

Doris Hostetler shook her head.

"Do you know where Sadie might be?" Ava asked one more time.

Doris dabbed at the corners of her eyes with a handkerchief. "I knew something bad would come of keeping secrets. I warned them."

Ettie leaned forward and patted Doris on her shoulder. "Who's 'them', Doris?"

Doris shook her head once more.

"You'd feel better if you unburdened yourself and told us exactly what's happened. Is it something to do with Horace's death?" Ettie asked.

Doris howled into her handkerchief at the mention of her son. Ettie knew that they could not ask her any more questions.

"Why don't I make us all some nice hot tea?"

Ava stood up.

Doris looked up at her.

"May I?" Ava asked.

Doris nodded.

It was another three hours before Ava and Ettie left Doris' house.

As the horse pulled the buggy down the tree-lined street, something occurred to Ettie. "It seems Horace told Sadie quite a bit of what was happening in his life. I wonder how she's involved in it all."

"I'm worried that she might be in danger."

Ettie scratched the side of her face. "There's always that possibility." A cold shiver ran through Ettie. "Anyway, Jeremiah should be finished with the floor by now."

"Good. Let's go and see how it looks," Ava said.

When they got back to the house, Detective Kelly was in his car waiting for them.

"Oh no. We forgot to go to the police station. He'll be here to ask me about that young man and also to take me to have a look at those mug shots. Leave the horse here and come with me?"

Ava and Ettie got out of the buggy and went straight to the detective who was still in his car.

"Afternoon, Detective," Ettie said through his car window.

"Good afternoon, ladies," the detective said. "We haven't been able to locate Sadie Hostetler. Mrs. Smith, I'd like you to come to the station to make an official report regarding the information you gave Crowley."

"I'll drive you, Ettie," Ava said.

"Thank you, dear." Ettie smiled at the younger woman.

"I also owe you an apology, Mrs. Smith."

"Oh?"

"About the key you found. It seems as though it belongs to a safe deposit box. We've taken it to the bank and they've told us that much."

"Crowley did say it was one of those keys."

"I'm afraid there's been another development, which might explain why your friend Sadie has disappeared."

Ettie leaned closer. "And what would that be?"

"While we were in the process of getting a warrant to open the safe deposit box, we discovered the box is held in the name of one Sadie Hostetler."

Chapter 14

Ettie looked at Ava, who looked just as shocked as she herself felt. Ettie rubbed her chin while she tried to make sense of the fact that the safe deposit box was in the name of Sadie Hostetler, Horace's sister. She had expected it to be in Horace's name or perhaps in the name of one of the gangsters. Maybe even in the name of Terence Wheeler.

Seeing the looks on their faces the detective said, "It came as a surprise to us as well."

"It seems odd, that's all. The key was found here, and I don't know that Sadie ever visited Agatha's house. Sadie kept to herself. I wonder if she opened the box because someone asked her to – or forced her – but why would she come around here looking for the key?"

"We won't know anything further, I guess, until Sadie returns," Ava said.

Ettie shook her head. "She told me some story

about someone telling her that Terence Wheeler hid the key with Horace's body. But how would Terence Wheeler have gotten the key from her? Did Sadie know Terence Wheeler to give him the key?"

"Well, we've got people on it." The detective looked at Ettie and narrowed his eyes. "Would you have any idea where Sadie Hostetler might be?"

Ettie raised her eyebrows, deepening the lines in her forehead. "I wouldn't have any idea. We've just come from her mother's place and she –"

Ava butted in. "She was very upset that Sadie's disappeared."

Ettie knew Ava's quick thinking just saved Mrs. Hostetler being interrogated by the police; the woman was in no state for that.

"When do you think you'll get the warrant?" Ettie asked.

"I'm hoping for tomorrow, once all the paperwork's done. I'm hoping the judge will sign off on it. I'm certain he will."

"Do you want to come inside, Detective Kelly?"

Ettie asked, hoping he wouldn't ask any more questions.

He shook his head and his eyes glazed over. "I don't know where all this is headed, but we'll know more once we get into that box at the bank." The detective nodded his goodbye before he got into his car. Ava and Ettie stood side by side in silence and watched him drive away.

"Where could Sadie be?" Ettie asked Ava.

Ava shrugged her shoulders. "You know her better than I do."

Ettie pushed her front door open. Jeremiah was gone and the floor looked clean and polished.

"Back to normal," Ava said.

"Yes, back to normal." Ettie took a deep breath. She missed her friend, Agatha, but was glad that she wasn't here to live through the dramas that were unfolding. "It occurs to me that since Sadie and Horace were so close, he had Sadie go to the bank and open a box. Horace is the connection between Sadie and the box."

"You think that's what happened? What if she

wanted to open a box for herself?"

Ettie scrunched up her nose. "For what?"

"Jah, I see what you mean. She wouldn't have had any valuables or anything to hide, not while she was one of us plain folk."

"He must have persuaded her to do it. Or someone else got her to do it. I guess we won't know until she tells us."

"Why wouldn't Horace have leased a box for himself? Would Horace have been involved in shady business?"

Ettie scratched her neck. Ava was right; if Horace had Sadie open the box, it meant that he was involved in some crooked business. That was not the Horace she remembered. "I don't know anymore. Nothing makes sense."

"Like the detective said, it'll make sense when we see what's in the box."

"Or when Sadie tells us. The best thing I can think of is that if Horace got involved with those crooked men somehow, or knew what they were up to, he might have put the stolen goods in there intending to notify the police."

"Ettie, do you think so? Really? He would've just taken it to the police station, wouldn't he?"

"*Nee,* they might have killed him for that."

Ava shook her head. "There are probably a thousand scenarios we could come up with. Do you think they'll find valuables in the box?"

Ettie nodded. "I do. Now, I'd hate to think that Horace was involved in anything dishonest, but we know from what Crowley and Sadie said that he knew criminals. He could very well have been involved in some way."

"*Jah,* in some way that ended up getting him killed. Do you think maybe his boss had him hide the stolen goods on his behalf?"

"We probably won't know until they open the box. They might be able to trace the stolen goods to the owner and then the police will be able to piece together what happened."

"Don't forget you have to go to the station to look at mug shots and make that report."

"That's right, and we might find out more if I

can identify the man who pointed that gun at me. I'll do it tomorrow."

* * *

When Ettie and Ava were approaching the police station the next day, they saw Sadie being walked into the station between two large police officers. Sadie had her head down and didn't see them.

"I hope she's all right. Do you think we should call her *mudder?*"

Ettie shook her head. *"Nee,* I don't think Doris can take any more upsets." Ettie sat down in a chair in the waiting area while Ava approached the officer at the desk to tell him why they were there. She was told that Detective Kelly was busy and they'd have to wait.

When Ettie saw that the officer didn't even make a move to tell him they were there, she walked up to him. "Please do tell the detective that we're here. I'm sure he'd like to know."

The officer stared at Ettie for a moment and then

said, "Very well. I'll let him know."

"Thank you kindly," Ettie said before she took a seat.

It was another fifteen minutes before the detective came out to speak to Ettie. "I'm sorry to have kept you so long, Mrs. Smith, but I've been run off my feet."

Ettie stood. "I saw Sadie being brought in. Is she all right?"

"We're just asking her a few questions. We found her at a bus station; she was leaving town."

"Could I speak to her?"

"I did ask if she wanted anyone present and she said no."

"I'm sure she'd want me there. Would you ask her if I could sit by her?"

Detective Kelly put his hands on his hips, and his mouth downturned. "I guess I could ask her. She's quite entitled to have someone with her at this stage, since she's only here for questioning."

"Thank you."

The detective disappeared down the long

corridor and a minute later, he beckoned Ettie from the corridor.

"I won't be long," Ettie said to Ava as she stood.

Ava replied, "Take your time; don't mind me."

Before Ettie entered the room where they were holding Sadie, the detective whispered to Ettie, "She says she has things to say that only a woman should hear."

Ettie pursed her lips and nodded before she entered the room and sat next to Sadie.

"Ms. Hostetler, I'm going to have a female officer sit in. I'll leave the room, but I'll be outside listening and as I've already said we'll be recording everything you say."

Sadie's mouth quivered as she nodded to the detective.

"Ms. Hostetler, the tape can't pick up body language or gestures. I'll say again, we'll be recording everything you say. You've heard that, and you understand?"

"Yes, Detective Kelly, I understand," Sadie said.

The detective continued, "I'll fetch the officer

now."

When the detective walked out, Ettie grabbed Sadie's hand. "Everything will be all right," Ettie said.

Sadie put her other hand over Ettie's and sniffed.

Detective Kelly returned with a young woman in a police uniform. "This is Officer Willis. Just tell her all that happened."

The young policewoman sat opposite Ettie and Sadie.

Sadie looked up at the detective. "So Ettie can stay? I'd feel better if she did."

"Yes, that's why she's here. And please, none of that Pennsylvania Dutch prattle, just speak in plain English."

Sadie nodded, then said, "Yes, Detective Kelly."

When the detective walked out, Ettie said, "Well?"

"I can barely speak. I haven't spoken of this in years."

Ettie waited in silence while Sadie composed herself.

"Would you like some water?" Officer Willis pushed a glass of water closer to her.

Sadie shook her head then stared at Ettie. "I'll start at the beginning."

"It's always best to start there," Ettie said.

"It was many years ago when I found out that Horace and I were expecting a child."

Ettie gasped, felt her throat constrict; then she felt she would be sick.

"Ettie, you knew we weren't real brother and sister, didn't you?"

Ettie's eyebrows flew up. She rubbed the side of her face. It had happened so long ago that she'd forgotten. The Hostetlers suddenly had a baby girl when Horace would've been just a baby himself. Horace and Sadie were the youngest of the children. The talk was that Sadie had been an unwanted baby from an unwed mother. She was raised along with their other children. "I knew, yes, I did, but it was so long ago. I had forgotten." Ettie put her hand to her fluttering stomach. Horace had been engaged to Agatha.

Sadie kept her eyes focused on the desk as though she couldn't look into the face of anyone who might judge her.

After clearing her throat and then taking a mouthful of water, Sadie continued, "He was to have gotten married to Agatha when we found out, and then he didn't know what to do. He knew he should marry me for the sake of the child. He said he had to get away from the community to clear his head. Agatha followed him, not knowing why he'd left so suddenly. He must have told her the truth of it all because she came back to the community not long after." She lifted her gaze to Ettie.

Ettie swallowed hard and tried to remain stony-faced. "Go on; what happened next?"

"While Horace was away, he went to work for a builder and he was a bad, bad man. I warned Horace – I just didn't trust the man."

"How did you know about him – the builder?"

"Just from things that Horace told me."

"So, you met with Horace regularly after he left the community?"

"About once a week," Sadie confessed. "After months went by, Horace still wouldn't marry me. I knew he loved Agatha, but I was the one having his *boppli.*" Tears trickled down Sadie's face.

"What happened then?" Ettie asked.

"I'll go back before then. I guess that wasn't the beginning. I'll go back to the very beginning." She cleared her throat again. "I was so young and was running around with Joshua Yoder, he said he wanted to marry me and we became secretly engaged. Then he told me days later he liked someone else." She looked up at Ettie with tear-filled eyes. "Joshua Yoder ended the relationship with me and then only one week later, he announced his engagement to Peggy Schroder. Why was our engagement a secret, but with Peggy he announced it straight away? I told Horace about it; he was my closest friend. Horace was comforting me, one thing led to another..."

"Well, we don't have to go into all that now," Ettie said, not wanting to know all the intimate details of the indiscretion.

"Okay, but I thought he loved me too, and then I found out that he didn't love me either. I thought he had changed his mind about Agatha just as Joshua had changed his mind about me." Sadie wiped her eyes.

Ettie wanted to say that Horace had crossed the line, especially when he was due to marry another. She shrugged off her judgmental thoughts. One indiscretion was as bad as another in God's eyes – she knew that to be true. She resisted the urge to shake sense into Sadie, but it was too late for that. The situation explained why Agatha never married Horace – she must have found out.

Sadie continued, "I went away for the birth; I hid my pregnancy right up to that time. Horace was there; he stayed with me for a week after William was born. Then I told him he had a decision to make. And I thought… I honestly thought he would choose me, and our baby. I wanted us to be married, be a real family, and then go back home after a few months with William."

Ettie wondered what had become of their baby.

Sadie looked down at her hands, which she was wringing in her lap. "Horace said he couldn't marry me. He came up with the idea that he'd have someone look after the baby for six months and then I would take him back home with me saying it was a relative's baby. I didn't want it to be that way, but Horace didn't care about that. He didn't care about me, not as much as he cared about her."

Ettie felt her pain, but even she didn't believe her next words. "I'm sure he did."

Sadie shook her head. "If he had, he would've married me. *Nee,* he wanted to be with Agatha – that was plain to see."

"What became of William?" Ettie finally asked.

Sadie looked into Ettie's face. "William is Bill Settler."

Ettie gasped. She added up the ages, the years, and it all fit. It was all possible, but could it be true? "Mr. Settler senior and his wife adopted him, then?"

Sadie shook her head. "They stole him from me. They agreed to look after him for six months.

That's what the arrangement was, but then when Horace went to collect him after the six months was up they wouldn't hand him over."

Ettie took a deep breath. All this happened right under her nose all those years ago and she hadn't known a thing about it. She'd always thought she knew all that happened in the community.

"At first, I didn't believe Horace. I thought he was lying because it would've been easier for him not to be bothered with the baby and to pretend he wasn't the boy's father. I went there myself, to the Settlers' house, and they wouldn't talk to me. They said that he was theirs now. I told them I was going to go to the police."

"And did you?" Ettie asked, trying to imagine large Bill Settler as a baby.

"No, because they told me the baby would end up in a home for unwanted children if I did that. Then they asked if I had money to fight a court case. They said it would cost me thousands and take years, and all that time William would be in the care of strangers who might treat him poorly."

"So they kept William and brought him up as their own?"

"They did. Horace was so angry. He said if he couldn't get the baby back for me legally, he'd play 'their game'. He knew the Settlers were into illegal goings on. He'd heard about their robberies and at one time they'd tried to get him involved. Mr. Settler told Horace that all his workers did 'jobs' for him. Horace refused to do anything of the kind. But then he stole from Mr. Settler and told him he could have the goods back when they gave William back, but they never did."

"And that's when Horace asked you to open a safe deposit box at the bank? To keep the goods he stole?"

Sadie nodded. "That's right. He came by one night, knocked on my window and handed me a black velvet bag. I opened it, the bag, to see what was inside. There were big diamonds and other stones. I thought they were too big to be real, but he assured me they were. There was a big diamond necklace, and packets of smaller diamonds and so many large ones. Then there were pretty red and green gems. They were so pretty; I couldn't take my eyes off them. I spread them all over my bed, I held them up to the light – they were beautiful things I'd never seen the like of."

"What did he have you do with them?" the officer asked.

"He said to go to the bank. He gave me a bundle of cash and said it would be enough to keep the box for a long time if need be. Then he told me exactly what to do and say when I got to the bank."

"And you followed his directions?" Ettie asked.

"I told him he should never have gotten involved with people like that. All of it was my fault."

"No, it wasn't. It wasn't your fault at all. Sometimes things happen and then bad things just follow and we're powerless to stop them." Ettie wasn't sure what she was saying, only that she was trying to comfort Sadie and help dull the pain that she'd obviously lived with for years. "Who was the man who pointed the gun at me? You seemed to know him."

"I haven't told you, have I?"

Ettie shrugged. "There's more?"

Sadie's mouth turned down and she took a deep breath. "Bill found out he wasn't a real 'Settler' and he set out to find Horace and me. Bill sought me out about three years ago. We meet every so often. He knows about the box at the bank – about it being in my name. He was trying to protect me by stopping the police from finding out. He wanted to get the key before the police found out the stolen goods were under my name at the bank."

"How was he trying to do that? By sending someone to get the key from me, from the house?"

Sadie nodded. "I guess so. I knew Bill would do something silly to protect me – we've developed a bond. Well, I've always had the bond, the connection with my child, but now it's different when he feels the same pull toward me."

"How did Bill know I had the key?"

"Eyes and ears, Bill calls them. He says he has them everywhere thanks to his *vadder* – I mean, father." Sadie corrected herself so the police could understand her.

Ettie knew that someone at the police station must have overheard mention of the key connected to Horace's murder.

Sadie continued, "I told Bill everything, about those people he calls his parents and how they tricked Horace and me."

Ettie wondered if Bill wanted that key for himself since the box held possibly half a million dollars' worth of gems, according to the Internet search.

"But they're the people who raised him, so I didn't want to say too many bad things about them," Sadie said.

"It must be hard for you, Sadie."

"It was heart-breaking. I used to sit outside his school whenever I had the chance. I watched him grow up from a distance."

The female officer asked, "You think that Bill, your biological son, was trying to protect you from the police? He had someone come to this lady's house with a gun? Is that correct?"

Sadie nodded. "I had stolen goods in that box."

"Why keep the stolen property all these years when the people refused to give the baby up?" the officer asked.

"I didn't," Sadie blurted out. "I didn't have the key. Horace told me that without the key you can't get into the box, and that's what they told me at the bank. They said if I lose the key they have to go through all kinds of legalities to get the box opened. I gave the key to Horace straight after I placed the goods in the box and I never saw him or the key again."

"Bill knew that there was a key somewhere, and knew what the box contained?" Ettie asked to confirm the events.

Sadie nodded.

The officer reminded her that she must speak her answers for the recording.

"Yes," said Sadie.

Ettie pulled her mouth to one side while she tried to figure it all out. "Horace took the diamonds as ransom so they'd give your baby back. If that had worked, you were going to take the baby back to the community, raise him yourself and tell everyone he was a close relative?"

Sadie nodded, caught herself, and then said, "Yes." She turned her attention to the female officer. "Will I go to jail?"

"I can't answer that." The officer stood. "I'll get Detective Kelly – I'm sure he'll have some more questions for you. I'm now leaving the room, and the recorder will be turned off."

When the officer walked out the door, Sadie leaned over and clasped Ettie's hand. "It's such a mess, Ettie, such a mess."

Ettie patted her hand. "Don't worry. It'll all get sorted out." Ettie heard the door open behind her. She turned to see the policewoman come back into the room.

"Detective Kelly is down at the bank."

"The warrant came through, then?" Ettie asked. She nodded.

"Do we just wait here?" Sadie asked.

"You can wait here or wait in a cell."

Sadie grimaced. "Here would be better."

Ettie frowned at the officer. "Is Sadie going to be charged with something? She's free to go, isn't she?"

"Not until Detective Kelly comes back." The woman turned and left the room.

Ettie looked back at Sadie and patted her hand again, wondering why the female officer had been so rude. She had seemed sympathetic earlier when she heard Sadie's sad story. "It'll all work out." Ettie held her mouth tight, hoping it would. "Do you have any idea who might have killed Horace?" Ettie asked Sadie.

"Agatha would've been angry to find out about the baby. Then there were Terence Wheeler and his people. Horace said that his boss had stolen the diamonds from Wheeler and his lot. They were the rightful owners of the diamonds. Well, not the rightful owners, because the goods were stolen."

"How did Horace get a hold of them, then? Wouldn't they have been in a safe or something?" Ettie asked.

"I don't know, I can't answer that. That's as

much as I know."

"You best tell Detective Kelly all that when he gets back."

Sadie nodded. "Oh, do you think I've got William into trouble now?"

"I guess they'll bring him in for questioning. I'm sure there's a law against sending someone somewhere with a gun." Ettie grimaced; Sadie sure did have a way of finding trouble.

Half an hour later, the detective walked through the door looking as though he'd been sucking on a lemon.

Both ladies waited for him to speak.

He planted both hands on the table and leaned over to Sadie. "We went to the bank, opened the box that was in your name and what do you think we found, Ms. Hostetler?"

"The diamonds?"

He shook his head. "Nothing. The box was empty."

Chapter 15

Sadie's face contorted. "That's not possible. I placed the diamonds in there myself and they said that no one but me could access it."

"Could Horace have taken the diamonds out? He had the key, after all," Ettie said.

The detective straightened up. "There's a lot you're not telling us, Ms. Hostetler." He pulled a piece of paper from his inner coat pocket. "I have here evidence that you accessed the box one month after you opened it."

"But that's not true. I didn't. I opened the box, paid the money and never went back. I gave the key to Horace straight after."

"I put it to you that Horace stole the gems from his employer, had you open the box, then you killed him and kept the stolen goods for yourself."

Ettie jumped to her feet. "Detective, that's not possible. It's simply untrue."

Sadie put her head in her hands and sobbed.

"Keep quiet, please, Mrs. Smith. You're only here out of respect to Detective Crowley."

"Yes, well, Detective Crowley would know to trust what I say."

"Sit down, Mrs. Smith," he said through gritted teeth. "Or you can wait outside."

Ettie sat, finding it hard to keep quiet.

Sadie sniffed back her tears and said, "It's not true. What you're saying is not true. I told Ettie the truth of what happened. He took the gems from Mr. Settler so they would give us our baby back, but they still wouldn't give him up. I went to the bank like Horace said to, then I gave him the key."

The detective sat down. He looked at both women, and said, "You had a baby with your brother that was brought up as a Settler?"

Ettie realized he must have missed some of Sadie's confession while he was at the bank with the warrant. "They weren't brother and sister, not by blood. Bill Settler, from Starling Homes, is Sadie and Horace's child. That's why Horace took the gems from Settler, so he would give him back the baby in exchange for the gems. The Settlers had agreed to look after their baby for six months, only then they wouldn't give him back."

The detective pulled his head back as though trying to absorb all the information. Then he looked at Sadie. "What Horace did was illegal, and you're an accessory to his crime."

Sadie pushed her lips together and then looked at Ettie with pleading eyes.

Ettie remembered from the Internet that the police couldn't make charges stick to Wheeler all those years ago due to lack of evidence. "An accessory to what, Detective? You said yourself the box was empty."

The detective glared at Ettie for a moment before his eyes traveled to Sadie. "This is by no means over, Ms. Hostetler, but I think we've kept you long enough today. We'll need to speak to you again."

The detective stepped back. Ettie put her arm around Sadie while she stood up. "Let's go, Sadie."

While Ettie and Ava ushered Sadie out of the

police station and into a taxi, Ettie recalled that the detective had forgotten about her looking at the mug shots and she still hadn't made a statement. Then she wondered what the detective would do now. Old Mr. Settler, the man who'd raised Bill, was dead, and so was Terence Wheeler.

On the way back to Sadie's house, Ettie's thoughts drifted to Bill Settler and the visit to his office. When Ava and I went there to find out about Horace he must have known all the while we were inquiring about his birth father. That also explains why his mother was irate to see him talking to us Amish folk since Sadie and Horace had been trying to get baby Bill back from her and her husband. She must have known that Bill had learned who his parents were.

When the taxi stopped at Sadie's house, Ettie asked Sadie, "Does your mudder know the truth of everything?"

"I told her some things years ago, but not everything. I couldn't hold the truth in any longer. It was my hope that by telling the truth Horace might come home."

"Truth of what?" Ava asked.

Sadie looked at Ava, then back to Ettie. "You can tell her, if you want. I suppose everyone will find out soon."

Ettie nodded. "Didn't you say that someone told you about Terence Wheeler? And something about hiding Horace's body and the key along with it?"

Sadie hid her face in her hands. "I made that up. I didn't want anyone to find out about the jewels in the bank. I don't want to talk about it anymore today."

Ettie was a little upset with Sadie. Here she was trying to help her and she wasn't helping herself. "Do you want me to come inside with you?" Ettie asked.

"*Nee. Denke* for everything you've done today, Ettie. Goodbye, Ava, and Ettie."

Ettie and Ava watched until Sadie disappeared into her house.

"Where to now?" the taxi driver asked.

Ava looked at Ettie who let out a long slow breath.

"Ava, what's the address of Starling Homes?"

"Really?" Ava raised her eyebrows.

Ettie nodded and then Ava gave the address of Starling Homes to the driver.

Ettie gave a laugh.

"What's so funny?"

"You've got a good memory."

Ava smiled. "I do for some things. What do you hope to find out by going to Starling Homes?"

"I'm hoping to talk to Bill."

"I guessed that much, but about what? And what did Sadie say you were allowed to tell me?"

Ettie took a deep breath and wondered where to start.

* * *

Bill Settler was locking his office when Ava and Ettie pulled up in the taxi. When he saw it was them, he gave a wave.

They hurried toward him as he gave a final turn of his key. When he spun to face them, he placed his keys in his pocket and said, "How can I help you ladies today?"

Ettie walked close to him. "Did you send someone over to my house to get a key? A man with a gun?" Ettie looked into Bill's face. She couldn't see any resemblance to Sadie, but he did have Horace's eyes, and his heavy frame. When he hesitated in answering, Ettie added, "Your birth mother seems to think that you did."

Bill's mouth fell open. He closed his mouth. "You'd better come inside and have a seat." He turned around, unlocked the door and pushed it open. "After you."

Ettie and Ava sat down.

When Bill was seated he asked, "You've spoken to my mother?"

"Which one?" Ava asked.

Ettie said, "We spoke to Sadie and she told us some interesting information."

"What do you want to know from me if Sadie's told you everything?"

Ettie bit on the inside of her mouth while she

wondered how to get some information out of him. "Did you send someone with a gun to get the key to the deposit box?"

He looked down at one of his large hands and dusted something off it with his other hand. "Guilty." Then he looked at Ettie. "She told me the box was in her name. I knew what was in the box because she'd told me about it."

"Do you mean what was supposed to be in the box?"

Bill drew his eyebrows together. "What do you mean?"

"The police got a warrant and when they opened the box today there was nothing inside. It was empty. They had a record of Sadie accessing the box a month after it was opened." Ettie could see he was genuinely surprised by the news. She hoped that meant his intentions had been good.

They all heard the sound of a car driving right next to Bill's office. He jumped to his feet when he saw it was the police. Ettie drew her mouth in a straight line and bit her lip. She knew they wanted to ask him about sending someone to her house with a gun. Sadie had said she was certain he'd sent that young man, and Bill had confirmed it.

"I'm sure they just want to ask you a few questions," Ettie said as she stood and pulled Ava to her feet. She knew Detective Kelly wouldn't be pleased about them being there. To Ettie's relief, it wasn't Detective Kelly that stepped out of the vehicle, but two uniformed officers.

"William Settler?" one of the uniformed officers asked as Bill stepped out of his office.

"That's me. What's all this about?"

"We've got some questions, and we'd like you to accompany us to the station."

"Very well. Give me a moment?" The policeman nodded. "I'll have to lock the office. Do you ladies want me to call you a taxi?"

"Yes, please," Ava said.

After Bill called for a taxi, he locked his office before heading to the police car with the policemen on either side of him.

As Ava and Ettie strolled to the front entrance,

Ettie whispered, "Looking at Bill walk away, I see he looks just like Horace. He's got the same large frame, and the same square shoulders."

"They're being polite to him. He doesn't look like he's in too much trouble."

"Not yet," Ettie said.

While they waited out the front for the taxi, Chad walked up to them. "Hello, again, Mrs. Smith." He nodded at Ava.

Ettie smiled. "Hello, Chad."

"Did my father just get taken away by the cops?"

"The police have some questions for him."

Ava added, "Yes, it's nothing to be concerned about."

Chad frowned. "Questions about what?"

Ettie breathed out heavily. "I'll let your father tell you."

Chad pulled a cell phone out of his pocket. "I'll call him and see what's going on."

Ettie looked up the road willing the taxi to hurry. "Let's go to my old house before we go to our place. I haven't seen Elsa-May in a while."

Chad had his head down still talking on his phone when the taxi arrived. Ettie looked back at him when she got inside the taxi but still, he didn't look up.

While Ava gave the driver directions, Ettie hit her fist on her forehead.

"Ettie! What are you doing?"

"What aren't we seeing, Ava?"

Chapter 16

"What aren't we seeing?" Ava repeated. "For one, it would be nice to know why Sadie doesn't remember going to that safe deposit box. Do you think she's got something wrong with her? I've read about people doing things and then they have no memory of it." Ava looked out the window of the taxi.

Ettie shook her head. "It's more simple than that, I'd say. What if it wasn't Sadie at all? What if it was someone who forged her signature? Crowley said they check the signatures against the ones held at the bank. All someone would have to do is dress in Amish clothes and write a signature that looks similar to Sadie's."

"They'd most likely need identification. Someone could have stolen her ID card and forged her signature, but who?"

"Not just who – how did they get the key back to Horace, since it seemed he was the last one to have it?" Ettie said.

"I can't believe she made up the story about Terence Wheeler hiding a body and a key," Ava said.

"Well, she admitted that was a lie."

"What else is she making up, then?"

Noticing that the taxi driver was leaning back toward them, Ettie said, "Let's finish this conversation when we're with Elsa-May."

* * *

After Ettie and Ava told Elsa-May everything that had happened, Ettie leaned forward. "I can't believe it. I mean I do, but it's so hard to believe. Poor Sadie's been through a bit. Nothing seems to work out for that girl."

"Well, what are your thoughts on everything, Elsa-May?" Ava asked.

"I'm shocked about Horace and Sadie, truly shocked." Elsa-May took a deep breath. "I knew she wasn't a Hostetler, but then there was the matter of Horace about to marry Agatha."

"I never would've thought it either, but what are your thoughts on the things besides that?" Ettie asked.

Elsa-May began by saying, "The money's gone–"

Ettie interrupted, delighted to be able to correct her sister. "It wasn't money, it was diamonds and gems."

Elsa-May narrowed her eyes at Ettie. "You know what I mean."

A giggle erupted from Ettie's lips.

"Ettie, this is serious." Elsa-May shook her head.

"I'm sorry, continue."

"Might I?" Elsa-May asked full of sarcasm.

Ettie nodded.

"As I was saying, the goods were gone from the box. Bill was maybe trying to help his birth mother, or maybe he was trying to get whatever was in that box for himself." Elsa-May turned to Ettie. "Who are the suspects?"

"Who killed Bill?"

Elsa-May gasped. "Is Bill dead too?"

"Nee, I meant to say Horace. You mean, who killed Horace?"

"Did the same person who took the gems kill Horace?" Ava asked.

Elsa-May and Ettie looked at each other.

Ettie was the first to speak. "I don't know, but it occurs to me that if Sadie didn't collect the goods from that box, it had to be a woman who did it, posing as Sadie."

Elsa-May placed her knitting back in the bag by her feet. "And who would have been the same age and who would have known about it?"

"Old Mrs. Settler, the one who raised Bill – although she wouldn't have been old back then. I think she would've been older than Sadie was, though, by maybe ten years. Mrs. Settler didn't want to give the baby up and she knew what Horace had stolen because he was using it as blackmail."

Ava added, "Jah, and she was very upset to see us there talking to Bill the first day we went there, wasn't she, Ettie?"

"She was, and she seemed to be talking as though Bill knew us. She could've thought I was his mother; that I was Sadie. All she would've seen is our Amish clothes from where she stood."

"You need to talk to Sadie again," Elsa-May said.

Ettie breathed out heavily. "Some things she just clams up about. Do you think we should go and talk to old Mrs. Settler, Bill's mother?"

Elsa-May said, "Most definitely."

"Ava, do you think you could find her address?"

"I do have a friend who works at the DMV. I'm certain I could get the address."

"Then we'll visit her tomorrow, if you can find where she lives by then."

* * *

Ettie knocked on Mrs. Settler's door with Ava standing next to her.

The door opened a crack with the security chain still attached. "What do you people want?"

"We'd just like to ask you some questions, Mrs. Settler. Bill's birth mother is a good friend of ours and she's just told us about him."

"And?"

"Could we talk to you? We won't take up much of your time."

The woman closed the door; they heard the clicking and sliding of the chain and then the door opened wide. "Come in, only if you're going to be brief." They followed Mrs. Settler through to a garden room at the side of the house. When they were seated, Mrs. Settler asked, "What do you want to know?"

Ettie licked her lips and looked over at Ava. She hadn't expected Mrs. Settler to speak to them, so she hadn't come prepared with questions.

Ava said, "Bill was given to you by an Amish couple?"

"They gave him to us and then they wanted him back." She folded her arms across her chest.

"They claim the arrangement was only for six months."

"No, it wasn't. They're lying. Anyway, Billy already told me he found his birth parents. Now he tells me that man – Horace – turned up dead."

"That's right," Ettie said. "He is deceased."

"Anyway, they lied to us. Bertram, that's my late husband, said they didn't want him. He said they couldn't have him because they were Amish and unmarried. That's what I was told and that's what I believe. There was nothing said about six months. I was upset that the woman came here wanting him back. Billy was happy and settled."

"Did you know about Bill's father taking money from your husband? I mean, not money – it was diamonds," Ettie asked.

"They said we could have him and then they changed their minds. How would you feel? We looked after him for months thinking we'd have him forever and then that man comes calling, trying to take him from us. After that, she turns up."

"Did your husband tell you Horace stole some things and tried to blackmail you?"

She looked at the two of them. "See, that Horace

wasn't an honest man. An honest man wouldn't have done that."

Ettie had to stop herself reminding Mrs. Settler about her husband's dubious reputation. It didn't escape Ettie's attention that the woman was the same height and weight as Sadie. She would've done anything to keep the baby, and that would include stealing back the diamonds that were used as blackmail against her. Did Mrs. Settler pose as Sadie at the bank?

Ettie didn't know whether it was old age causing her impatience or if she was simply frustrated by not knowing the truth. "Mrs. Settler, did you go to the bank posing as Sadie Hostetler and remove the gems from the safe deposit box?"

Mrs. Settler stared at Ettie with an open mouth before she said, "I certainly did not. How dare you accuse me of such a thing? You've got a thundering cheek."

"We're sorry, Mrs. Settler, but I'm sure the police are going to come and ask you the very same thing."

"They are? Do they think I killed him? I wouldn't do it. I wouldn't have killed my son's birth father even if he were a horrid man. Neither would I have stolen anything out of a deposit box – I wouldn't even know how to go about doing such a thing."

Just then, the three women heard cars screech to a halt outside the house. Mrs. Settler stood up and peered through the trellis of the garden room. From there she had a clear view to the front of her house. "It's the police." Tears fell down her face. "I'm not strong enough for all this. I've been through too much already."

"Did you kill Horace, Mrs. Settler?" Ettie asked.

She hung her head. "No, but I know who did."

Chapter 17

Before Mrs. Settler could tell Ettie and Ava who killed Horace, the police were at the door.

When she opened the door, Detective Kelly looked straight at Ettie, who was standing behind her. He frowned and then looked back at Mrs. Settler. "We'd like to ask you a few questions, Mrs. Settler."

She folded her arms and leaned against the doorframe. "About?"

"I'm sure you'd prefer to discuss the matter in private."

"Is Bill in some kind of trouble?"

"Mrs. Settler, can we come inside?" the detective persisted.

"No, I have nothing to say."

She closed the door on both the detective and the officer who was standing beside him. Ettie had never seen anyone so bold as Mrs. Settler. But then, since her husband had been a villain, she wouldn't have much respect for the law.

Mrs. Settler turned back to Ettie. "Where were we?" Before Ettie could speak, Mrs. Settler looked through the peephole at the police. "Good – they're going." Mrs. Settler walked back to the garden room and sat down.

Ettie followed after her, and when she was seated, she asked, "You said you know who killed Horace? "

Mrs. Settler looked down at the terracotta tiles on the floor.

Ettie ran through all the suspects in her mind to see if she could guess the name in the seconds before the woman spoke. There were Sadie, Agatha, Mr. Settler senior and Terence Wheeler, or one of his men.

"I'm certain it was that woman."

"Which woman?" the two women said at the same time.

"The woman who gave us the baby and then wanted him back."

Ettie pulled a face and then stared at Ava.

"Now you both must go. It's just too much for me."

Ettie knew she'd get no more out of the woman. "Thank you for telling us all that you have, Mrs. Settler."

She led them back to the front door.

Once they were outside, they walked up the road hoping to find a taxi.

"Kelly wasn't happy to see me. I think we should go straight to the station, make that report and look at those mug shots."

"Ettie, don't you ever get tired? Or hungry?"

"Jah, I could eat."

Ava smiled. "I was hoping you'd say that." Ava pulled her in the direction of a small coffee shop that she'd sighted down at the end of the street.

When they were seated with coffee and bagels, Ettie said, "I'm sorry to drag you into all this, Ava."

Ava smiled. "I have to help to clear Agatha's name. Do you still think the detective thinks she had something to do with it?"

Ettie finished the mouthful she was chewing.

"Not now. Not since all this has come to light about the key, and then Horace and Sadie having a child together."

Ava took a sip of coffee. "They could think that Agatha was upset with him for what had happened between him and Sadie and then she hit him over the head."

"People have killed for less, I suppose. At least now the police have a few more things to sort out. At the beginning it was only Agatha, and now they've many more people to consider."

Ava stared into the distance.

"What are you thinking?"

"Oh, Ettie, how can you ever trust a man? I'm shocked about Horace and Sadie – it just seems so awful. There's Agatha, thinking she would marry Horace and have a family with him, and then she finds out he's having – or has had – a *boppli* with someone Agatha would have considered as Horace's *schweschder*. It's all so awful, too awful."

"It is, but so are many things in life. It's how we deal with these challenges that's important. We can't judge – it's not up to us to do that."

Ava nodded, then stared into her coffee.

"Why have you never married, Ava? You must be about twenty five now."

"Twenty three. It just seems marriage is for other people. I haven't met a man who makes me feel that I can totally be myself when I'm with him."

"What about Jeremiah?" Ettie said with a twinkle in her eye. "He'd be over twenty now, I'd say. I've got so many great nieces and nephews it's hard to keep up."

"He does seem nice, but he's never been anything more. I mean, he's never asked me to spend time with him, so I don't know how I could get to know him better. I feel too old to go to the singings – they're more for the younger people."

"Why don't Elsa-May and I have you two to dinner?"

Ava giggled. "Ettie, don't you dare do that. It'll be so obvious that I'd be embarrassed."

Ettie pouted. "If you want something to happen, Ava, you have to do something about it. You can't just sit down and hope that a man will come to you if that hasn't happened already."

"Forget I said anything. I'm okay as I am. I'm happy living alone."

Ettie raised her eyebrows at her and Ava looked away.

"The greatest joy in my life was having a family. Seeing the miracle of birth as the little ones come into the world – there's nothing like it."

"I've got my horse, and thanks to you, now I've got chickens."

Ettie giggled, and covered her mouth with her hand as she burst into all-out laughter.

Ava giggled too. "Besides, Agatha seemed happy and she never married."

"That's true; we can find happiness wherever we are." Ettie patted her mouth with the paper napkin. "Ah, that was nice. *Denke* for suggesting it. Now, are you ready to face Detective Kelly?"

"It's you who'll have to do that," Ava said with a smirk.

* * *

Ettie approached the sergeant at the front desk. "I'm Ettie Smith. Detective Kelly has been waiting on me to look at some photographs and to make some kind of a report."

With just a glance up at her, the sergeant picked up the phone and talked to the detective. "I've got a Mrs. Smith here to make a report and look at some photos." When he hung up the receiver he said, "Follow me."

Ava sat in the waiting area while Ettie followed the gruff sergeant into an empty room. An officer came in and took down her statement over what happened when Sadie visited her. When she was done with that, she had to look through a series of photographs. She was unable to identify the young man with the gun.

"Is that all for today?" Ettie asked, hoping she could leave.

"Detective Kelly would like a word with you."

That was what Ettie had feared. She waited while the officer went to fetch the detective.

When he came in, he sat before her and said,

"What were you doing at Mrs. Settler's house?"

She opened her mouth to speak when he raised his hand to stop her. "I know exactly what you were doing. You were asking her questions. And if it weren't for you, she would've spoken to us when we got there."

"No, I'm sure –"

"Mrs. Smith, I could have you arrested for obstructing justice."

"But I –"

"There have been some developments."

Ettie raised her eyebrows. Had they found out some things from Bill Settler?

"Since you insist on sticking your nose in where it doesn't belong, have you found out anything?"

Ettie scratched her neck, not sure what she should reveal. "I know a great many things about a lot of people, but I'm not sure which of it would be of interest to you."

"I'll tell you something and then you might see how vital it is that you stay out of my way. After we got a warrant for Mrs. Settler's bank accounts, we found that exactly a week after the box in Sadie's name was accessed, over three hundred thousand dollars was deposited into her account."

Ettie raised her eyebrows. "Really?"

"Yes, really. We'll also be charging Bill Settler. He admitted to sending someone to your house with a gun to get a key from you."

"How would he have known?" Ettie asked.

The detective ignored Ettie's question. "A warrant for Mrs. Settler's arrest has just come through – that is, if she hasn't already been spooked by your visit and disappeared. Our plan was to visit her and talk to her about what her son had said, hoping the warrant would come through while we were with her. But you ruined that for us. We'll have to hope that she's still at the house."

"You could've had her watched."

"Manpower, Mrs. Smith, manpower – it's not an unlimited resource."

"I'm sorry, Detective. I didn't mean to get in the way. I'm just trying to clear my friend's name. She'd do the same for me."

The detective stared at her blankly as though he wanted to admonish her some more.

"I should go, I suppose. I've looked at the photos and I've made that report."

"Very well. Please stay out of this whole thing, Mrs. Smith. I know you're trying to help your friend and I can understand that, but you are getting in our way."

Ettie rose to her feet and gave him a nod. She left the detective sitting and hurried out to meet Ava in the waiting area.

Chapter 18

"It doesn't add up, Ettie. There are too many things that just don't make sense," Ava whispered to Ettie behind a cupped hand so the taxi driver wouldn't overhear.

"I've been thinking that myself. Sadie's been lying, so what else has she lied about?"

"Do you think she was the one who went to the box?"

"Nee. Why would she come looking for the key, then? And then there's all that money that appeared in Mrs. Settler's account." Ettie scratched the side of the cheek. "Let's talk to Sadie some more, shall we? I'm going to pretend we have some information about her. Just follow my lead."

Ava leaned over and gave the driver Sadie's address.

The taxi stopped in front of the house and as Ava paid the driver, Sadie came outside and walked toward them.

"Can we talk, Sadie?" Ettie asked.

"Mamm's asleep. She's been very upset about everything. Mind if we sit on the porch so we don't wake her?"

Ettie and Ava followed Sadie to the porch. When they were seated, Ettie began by saying, "Sadie, it's been found out that it was you who went back to the safe deposit box."

Sadie looked down at her hands in her lap and remained silent. Just as Ettie was about to continue speaking, Sadie said, "I did it for my baby. It was my last chance. I thought if the Settlers could see all those diamonds and everything they could have, then they would give me back my baby."

"You got everything out and took it to them?" Ava asked.

Sadie nodded. "Mr. Settler wasn't home. Mrs. Settler said she wouldn't give the baby back for all the money in the world. I tried to make her see that he was my baby and I loved him more than she would ever be able to imagine. I said I'd go to the police, and then she said I'd go to jail for stealing."

She looked at Ettie with tears brimming in her eyes. "What use would I be to my son if I was in jail? It was Horace's fault; he'd made another mistake involving me in robbery."

"What happened to the gems you took out?"

Sadie shrugged. "I knew I couldn't get my baby back. Horace was useless and I couldn't go to the police, and I had no money for a lawyer."

"Why didn't you go to the bishop?" Ava asked.

"What? Then I'd be shunned and where would I go? I don't think the community would've been able to help me." Sadie looked into her palms. "I left the gems with the woman whom my son would grow up to call his mother. They were no good to me if they weren't going to get my son back. I wondered if I should sell them to pay for a lawyer to get him back, but they were stolen goods and I might have gone to jail if I was caught."

"You gave Mrs. Settler the gems?"

"I made her promise that she would always take care of William. She promised me that, and they kept his name – his first name. She said she would open an account with the money the gems brought in and the money would be for William. She said she wouldn't tell a soul of it. Not her husband, not William –no one. She asked me to stay away from them and I agreed."

"Then you left and forgot about him – or tried to forget?" Ava asked.

"I could never forget my *boppli,* never. He was everything to me."

"Don't say another word, Sadie."

All heads turned to see Mrs. Doris Hostetler at the front door. Sadie flew to her feet. *"Mamm,* go back to bed."

"Nee, don't say another word."

"It's too late for that. It'll all come out now."

Ettie leaned closer.

"Ettie and Ava, please leave my property."

Ettie looked at Sadie. "Why did you pretend to be shocked when the police found nothing at the bank?"

"Don't say anything, Sadie," Doris ordered.

Sadie turned away from them.

"I've asked you both to go."

Ava and Ettie stood up, walked down the steps and headed to the main road. Ettie looked back to see Sadie's head hanging low as her mother spoke crossly to her.

"What do you make of that?" Ava asked Ettie.

"It explains a few things."

"But not who killed Horace."

Once they got off the Hostetler property and onto the main road, they saw a buggy heading toward them.

"I wonder who this'll be," Ettie said.

"I think it's Jeremiah."

Ettie's face lit up.

"Don't you dare say anything, Ettie. Don't invite him anywhere or anything like that. Ettie?"

Ettie nodded.

"What are you doing out this way?" Jeremiah said as he stopped the buggy.

"We were visiting Sadie," Ava said.

"And you're going to walk five miles home?"

Ava and Ettie looked at each other. They couldn't

tell him they were just ordered off the property and didn't have a chance to ask to call a taxi from the phone in the barn.

"Are you going our way?" Ettie asked.

"Looks like I am now."

They got into Jeremiah's buggy.

"Aunt Ettie, do you like the floorboards as they are? I could put a varnish on them and have them shiny."

"They're good as they are. You must let me know what I owe you for doing all that work."

"*Nee,* I'll not charge one of my own."

"It took you too long to do and I want to pay you for your time, the same as you'd charge anyone else. That's fair."

"*Nee,* aunty. I'll not do it."

"You must come to dinner then, at my old house with Elsa-May. We'll cook up a *wunderbaar* meal."

"That I'll say yes to." Jeremiah turned to Ettie and Ava in the back seat and smiled.

"You come too, Ava."

Ava dug Ettie in the ribs. "I've been fairly busy

these days, helping mum get things ready for the markets."

"Come on, Ava. You can spare just one night, can't you? I'll fetch you and bring you home," said Jeremiah.

Ettie looked at Ava with a huge grin and nodded.

While frowning at Ettie, Ava said, "Well, I'll see if I can."

Chapter 19

It was the next day that Crowley knocked on the front door of Agatha's old house.

"Come in," Ettie said. "Tea?"

"Always." He followed Ettie to the kitchen. "The floor looks much better."

"It does, thanks to my great nephew." As she put the pot on the stove and lighted the gas, she asked, "Have you been following what's happened?"

He nodded as Ettie sat at the kitchen table opposite him. "Kelly's interview with Mrs. Settler revealed some interesting things, which led to Sadie being brought in for questioning earlier today. She admitted to giving Mrs. Settler the goods from the deposit box, which means she's also admitting to being the one to take the goods out of the box."

"Yes, and she denied that up until now." To avoid another lecture, Ettie did not tell Crowley that she'd been to see Sadie the day before.

Crowley said, "She lied about going to the box

the second time and she lied about someone telling her that Terence Wheeler hid Horace's body along with a key."

"What did Mrs. Settler have to say, exactly?"

"She said Sadie gave her the money for her son and said that Horace was gone, which leads me to believe that Sadie knew who killed him, or at least knew he'd been killed."

"She did say at one point that Horace told her he was heading north. She might just have meant 'gone' as in 'never coming back'."

"That's true."

"Anyway, can you believe what Mrs. Settler says? The woman stole Sadie's baby."

The retired detective heaved a sigh. "According to Sadie, she didn't give the baby back after six months, but according to Mrs. Settler, that was never the arrangement. How do we know that Horace didn't tell the Settlers one thing, and tell Sadie another?"

"That's what I've been thinking, but if that had been the case then why would he have been blackmailing the Settlers to get him back?"

"He could've changed his mind once he saw how upset Sadie was. He might have realized he'd made a huge mistake and tried to right his wrong," Crowley said.

Ettie tapped her fingers on the table. "That could very well be the case." The sound of the water boiling drew Ettie's attention. She rose to her feet to make the tea. "I can offer you fruit cake?"

"Just the tea will be fine, Ettie, thanks."

"Elsa-May made the fruit cake."

"Did she? I'll just have a small piece, then."

Ettie chuckled. The detective did like his food, and anything Elsa-May made was always a winner. Ettie cut two small slices of cake while the tea steeped. "There you go." She sat again once she'd placed the tea and cake on the table. "It's hard to know who's lying and who's telling the truth."

"Each woman was convinced that the baby should've been with her. I don't think we'll ever know what Horace arranged."

Ettie blew on her tea. "Poor Sadie. Horace left

and she didn't have him or her baby."

Crowley took a small bite of cake.

"Something's just occurred to me." She stared into the distance.

He swallowed his cake and said, "What is it?"

"If Sadie admits to taking the goods out of the box, doesn't that put her in the possession of the key? And the key was found with the body."

"But not on the body. If it had been on the body, then that would have been incriminating, but it wasn't."

Ettie breathed out heavily and placed her teacup back into the saucer. *Did Agatha leave me her house hoping I'd find Horace's murderer? But that would've meant she knew he was under the house. How odd that, for all those years, she sat on the rocking chair in the middle of the floor, directly over him.*

"What are you thinking, Ettie?"

He jolted her out of her daydreams. "Just thinking, and wondering, what became of the key after Sadie went to the bank. If she had it then, what became of it? She lied about Terence Wheeler hiding a key with Horace's body. Did she give the key to Horace at some point after she took the gems out? She did say that Mrs. Settler agreed to keep the matter of the money to herself."

"Ettie!"

"What?"

"You spoke to Sadie? You knew about this?"

Whoops! "Well, yes, I did speak to Sadie before she spoke to the police about it. I went to see her yesterday and she admitted some things, but then her mother came to the door and asked Ava and me to leave. I didn't tell you when you first arrived because I knew you'd tell me to keep out of things."

"Ettie."

"I know, I know. I've already gotten into trouble from Detective Kelly about talking to people. Please don't tell him."

He shook his head. "I'll have to think about that." He took the last bite of cake.

Ettie put her teacup to her lips and took a small sip then lowered it to the table. "She can't have been telling the truth about anything. She admits taking the money, so she would've had the key. If she did have it, then she knew about Horace being under the floor because the key was hidden close by him. Although she'd taken the gems out, so I suppose she didn't want the key found because it was in her name and would possibly link her with stolen goods. Perhaps she thought it would make her look less guilty if someone else had gone and taken the gems out. She could've wanted the police to think someone posed as her."

"What was Agatha's involvement, then? This is her house."

"*That* we'd only find out from Sadie's lips."

"You need to tell the police what you know, Ettie."

"I don't know anything that the police don't know now." Ettie pulled a face. She hadn't exactly made best friends with the new detective.

"You know a lot, and if you tell Kelly everything there might be some tiny piece of evidence that you don't know you have."

Ettie gulped. "Will you come with me?"

"I'll drive you."

Ettie looked at the empty cups and the crumbs on the plates. "Will I have time to do the dishes and freshen up?"

Crowley stood. "I'll take care of the dishes while you freshen up. Then I'll call ahead and let him know we're coming."

* * *

Crowley and Ettie waited in an interview room for Detective Kelly.

"I need to warn you, he's not happy with me," Ettie said. "Don't leave me alone with him."

Crowley smiled. "He'll be all right."

Kelly came through the doorway with a large folder and kicked the door closed behind him with a backward flick of his foot. He nodded hello to both of them before he sat on the other side of the large table.

Kelly began by saying, "What we know so far,

Mrs. Smith, is that Sadie has admitted to taking the stolen goods back out of the safe deposit box. She claims she lied about it in the beginning because she knew the goods were stolen and she thought she'd be charged." He murmured, "Which is still to be decided." He went on, "We have a confession from Mrs. Settler that she accepted the stolen goods from Sadie Hostetler, sold them, and then placed the money in an account for her son."

Ettie closed her eyes. Did Sadie say that she sold the gems and gave the money to Mrs. Settler? She couldn't be certain of that so she remained silent on the matter.

Crowley added, "That places the key in the possession of Sadie Hostetler."

"Which was found near the body," Kelly said. Crowley nodded as Kelly stood and said, "I'll get a warrant prepared for her arrest."

"What?" Ettie pushed herself to her feet. "Don't you want to hear everything I know so you might be able to find a clue somewhere?"

Kelly exchanged glances with Crowley before

he sat down. He scratched his head in an agitated manner, then said, "Look, Mrs. Smith, I'm grateful that you're trying to be helpful, but I don't have time to listen. Haven't you told me everything you know already?"

Crowley said, "Since Ettie – Mrs. Smith – knows everyone involved, she could very well know something that could be vital to the case."

Detective Kelly closed his eyes. "If you'll wait here, I'll be back in a moment. I'll have someone else pick up Sadie Hostetler."

When he was out of the room, Ettie asked Crowley, "Do they have enough information – I mean evidence – to arrest her?"

He nodded. "She was in possession of stolen goods and that can be proven when we find out where the goods were liquidated."

"Don't they have to find that out first?"

"Just trust the process, Ettie."

Ettie couldn't help scowling at Crowley. He's the one who got her there to talk to Kelly and Kelly obviously had no interest in what she had to say.

What could she tell them that they hadn't already found out? Ettie stood up. "I'm old and I'm tired. I don't think that man wants to listen to anything I have to say, and quite frankly, I'm annoyed by the whole thing."

Crowley jumped to his feet. "Don't be like that, Ettie."

"Would you mind driving me home?"

He breathed out heavily. "You wait here, I'll find Kelly and tell him we're leaving."

"He won't be upset about that," Ettie murmured under her breath. Once Crowley was out of the room, she sat back down and studied her surroundings. The large mirror on the wall reflected the sterile gray interior. Was that a two-way mirror? She wondered if someone on the other side was watching her. But who would want to listen to what she had to say, or look at an old lady? She wasn't guilty of any crime and hadn't done anything wrong, so surely there'd be no one behind that mirror. Not knowing if there was anyone behind it unnerved her.

Ettie walked into the corridor and opened the

door to the room next-door. She peeped in to see that it was empty and it was not the door that led to the other side of the mirror.

Just as she was closing the door she heard Kelly's voice behind her. "I hear you want to leave now?"

Ettie jumped and saw Kelly right there with Crowley a little way behind him. "Yes, I'm a little tired. Maybe I could come back and talk to you another day?"

"I'll look forward to it," he said in a sarcastic tone.

"Let's go, Ettie."

Ettie followed Crowley out of the building.

When they were outside, he turned to her. "What were you doing in that other room?"

"Do you think Kelly noticed?"

"I think he's got so much on his mind that he didn't recall which interview room we were in."

Ettie relaxed. "That's good."

"Well?"

"I was just wondering if there was anyone behind the two-way mirror."

Crowley's stern face softened into a smile. "It's accessed from a room on the other side of the building. And I don't think there would've been anyone interested enough in what we had to say to watch us."

"That'd be true enough. Detective Kelly seemed most put out at the thought of having to listen to me tell him everything I knew."

"Yes, I'm sorry about that, Ettie. That's not the way I would've done things. Everyone has their own way of doing things, I guess."

Ettie nodded.

"Well, come on. The car's this way."

Chapter 20

Ettie had Crowley drive her back to Agatha's old house. She stood at the door and watched Crowley drive away. A quick look in the paddock told Ettie that Ava had taken her buggy somewhere. At last she could have a time to sit in peace and empty her mind of all the dreadful things she'd heard.

She had kept the door locked since she'd had the incident with the intruder who'd ripped up her floor. She reached into her sleeve and pulled out her front door key, pushing it into the lock and turning it. Once she pushed the door open she stepped inside, hoping that everything was okay.

She took a few steps further, slowly, until she saw that nothing was out of place. After she checked every room she finally felt she was able to relax. She kicked off her boots, placed her slippers on her feet and headed to the kitchen. Ettie smiled when she saw how tidy Crowley had left things in the kitchen – even the dishtowel was carefully folded and left adjacent to the sink. After she made a cup of tea, Ettie headed to the living room.

Ettie looked around – it didn't feel like her house. It would always be Agatha's home. She sat in Agatha's rocking chair holding her teacup, careful not to spill a drop. After looking around the room, she put the cup to her lips. She slurped her tea, glad that Elsa-May wasn't there to tell her to stop. Hot tea tasted much better when it was slurped. "Did you play a part in this nasty business, Agatha?" she asked her late friend, wishing Agatha could tell her exactly what she knew. Agatha had to have known something about Horace being under the floor, Ettie was now convinced of that.

A knock on Ettie's front door startled her. She hadn't heard anyone approach the house. She set her tea down on a small side table and peeped out one of the front windows. It was Sadie. *The police are going to think I'm meddling again.*

With Sadie sobbing as she waited for the door to open, Ettie had no choice but to let her in. Once the door was open, Sadie put her arms around Ettie's shoulders and sobbed. Ettie instinctively patted her on the back.

"Oh, Ettie. I'm so upset."

"Come inside. I've just boiled the water." As Ettie closed the front door she looked up the road. No sign of the police.

She sat Sadie at the kitchen table while she made her a cup of tea. "Do you want to tell me what's going on, Sadie? I was at the police station earlier today and I believe I heard them saying they're getting a warrant for your arrest."

Sadie sniffled and shook her head. "I don't care anymore. I don't care what happens to me now. My life is finished."

Ettie placed a cup of tea in front of her. "Did you come to talk to me?"

"I don't know what to do."

"You could start by telling the truth before the police think you had something to do with Horace's murder."

Sadie's eyelids flickered as she avoided Ettie's

gaze. Ettie wondered if she did have something to do with his death. "Correct me if I'm wrong, Sadie. Horace gave you the stolen goods and had you open the deposit box at the bank. You never gave him back the key, did you?"

Sadie sniffled, closed her eyes and said, *"Nee."*

"You heard Horace was returning to the community to marry Agatha. You were furious; he was the cause of you losing your baby so you wanted to confront him. You drove past and saw he was here at Agatha's house. You came to the door to talk to him, possibly to tell Agatha about the baby you'd had with Horace. You hit him hard in anger and killed him."

With both hands clutching her stomach she asked, "Did Agatha tell you?"

Ettie slowly shook her head. "Agatha kept your secret. Although she loved him, he'd betrayed her as well as you. She couldn't have been happy with what he'd done. Neither could she marry him."

Sadie sighed. "It's just as you said. Only Agatha was right here when I hit him, and she saw the whole thing. I didn't mean to kill him. I was so upset with him and how he'd trusted those people with William. He'd lost me my baby because he wouldn't do the right thing and marry me."

Ettie patted her on the arm.

Sadie continued, "Agatha knew it was an accident and that's why she helped me hide his body. We figured nobody would find him there. We had a pact, Agatha and I. We didn't like each other, but we had both loved Horace. We made certain to stay a distance from one another after that, in the hope that no one would suspect that we had worked together to create his disappearance."

"Did Horace know you cleared out the safe deposit box?"

Sadie shook her head. "It was after Horace had gone and I realized I was never going to get my baby back. It was me who took the gems out of the bank. I sold all that I could – there were some that were too big to sell quickly. I took the big diamonds and the cash to Mrs. Settler hoping that when she saw all that money and those big diamonds she'd give me my baby. When I realized she wouldn't give my baby up for anything, I left everything with her. What else could I do? That was all I could do for him; the last thing I could do for him."

"It must have been hard for you to keep that secret all these years."

"It was. I told mamm some of it."

"What happened to the key after that?"

"I gave the key to Agatha and asked her to hide it where no one would ever find it."

"Ah, and she hid it close to Horace."

"She never told me where she hid it. When I heard that Horace was found I asked Bill to help me find the key. I knew that the police would've combed the place and if they found the key it'd be only a matter of time before they pieced everything together. I had to tell Bill about the box and that I might go to jail if they found out that key was in my name. He came here the other night to look for it, but he told me someone spotted him. Then he heard that you had the key and he sent someone to get it."

"He was doing what he could to take care of you, Sadie."

"Now I've probably gotten my own son into trouble."

Ettie heard cars pull up in front of her house. She walked to the front window and pulled the curtain aside. She called out to Sadie who was still in the kitchen. "It's the police – looking for you, no doubt."

Sadie rose to her feet and joined Ettie by the front door. "I'm ready for them."

Ettie opened the door just as Detective Kelly was walking up the porch steps followed by two policemen.

The detective looked past Ettie to Sadie. "Sadie Hostetler, I have a warrant for your arrest."

She stepped forward and Ettie noticed one of the policemen had handcuffs in his hands. He stepped forward. "Put both of your hands out."

"Is that necessary, Detective?" Ettie asked. "She's not going to run off anywhere."

"Very well." The detective gave the officer a

look, which caused the officer to clip the cuffs back onto his belt. "Let's go, Ms. Hostetler."

"Will you be all right, Sadie?" Ettie called after her.

"I'll be fine, Ettie. I'll tell them all that I told you."

The detective looked up, stopped in his tracks, turned around and glared at Ettie.

Ettie took a step back, wondering what she should say. Before anything came to mind, the detective turned again and continued to the waiting car.

* * *

With all that had happened that day, Ettie decided that Agatha's house held too many sad memories, and so she went back to stay with Elsa-May that night.

After dinner, while she was doing her needlework and Elsa-May was knitting quietly, Ettie remembered her words to Jeremiah. "I told

236

Jeremiah we'd have him over for dinner. And I invited Ava over too."

Elsa-May looked over the top of her glasses. "No good comes from meddling in other people's lives, Ettie."

"It's just dinner. Whatever the two of them do after that is none of my business."

Elsa-May scoffed. "You make it sound like they're going to run off and do something bad."

"You know that's not what I mean. Once they get to know one another a little better they might find that they like each other."

"And if they do it's well and good." Elsa-May nodded firmly.

Ettie smiled and looked back at her needlework as she planned what they'd cook for the dinner. "Perhaps we should have that dinner next week?"

Elsa-May kept her head down. "Whenever you'd like; a week or more would give us enough time to plan for a nice dinner."

Chapter 21

The next day, after completing their chores, Elsa-May and Ettie had settled down for a quiet day when someone knocked on their door.

"I'll get it." Ettie rose to her feet and hurried to the door, hoping it would be someone from the community coming with news of Sadie. She'd not been brave enough to go near Detective Kelly since he'd arrested Sadie the day before.

"Ah, I'm glad it's you. Come in." Ettie ushered Crowley through the door and sat him in the living room.

"Thank you, Ettie. That's one of the best receptions I've ever gotten."

"Ettie's been anxiously waiting to find out what happened to Sadie. Is she still arrested?"

Ettie didn't mind Elsa-May speaking on her behalf today. She looked at the retired detective, waiting, hoping he knew something.

"I've just come from the station. Sadie was

arrested for the murder of Horace Hostetler after her confession. Her son, Bill Settler, posted bail."

"She's out?"

Crowley nodded.

"Will she go to prison?" Elsa-May asked.

Crowley sucked in his lips before he said, "She didn't have the intention to kill him and there were extreme circumstances, but I guess it depends on the judge and the jury on the day. With the waiting periods it might be two or three years before she stands trial."

"What about Mrs. Settler? She took what Sadie gave her; will she be charged?"

"I'm not certain, but most likely she'll be charged. They're still sorting through the evidence."

"Well, you were right about one thing, Ettie," Elsa-May said.

"I was right about a lot of things." Ettie glared at her sister. She reckoned she'd done pretty well piecing everything together.

"I meant you were right about Agatha not killing Horace."

"There was never any doubt in my mind about that." Ettie smiled, feeling good that her sister had finally given her a compliment. "I knew Agatha had no violence in her, but keeping a secret, that would be something she'd do. She was a good and loyal friend these past ten years, since we grew close."

"The Settler family's not short on money, I can assure you of that. With Bill looking after her, Sadie will get the best legal team money can buy."

"The son now looks after the mother that never got a chance to look after him," Elsa-May said, her voice filled with sadness.

"It's awful for Sadie that she lost a son. It would've been sad for Agatha too, but she didn't lose a child, just a man. There were many others she could've chosen over the years." Ettie wiped away a tear.

"That's what secrets will do. What would've happened if Sadie had been able to tell the truth about having a baby? Surely what she would've gone through would be less painful than what

241

finally happened?" Crowley asked.

Ettie and Elsa-May looked at each other. "Most likely they would have had to have confessed their sin in front of the community on a Sunday, in front of everyone."

"Would they have been shunned?" Crowley asked.

"Depends if they'd been baptized or not. The young usually wait until just before marriage to get baptized," Elsa-May said. "They would've had to live with the shame. And they'd have had to marry."

"It probably all came down to Horace not wanting to marry Sadie," Crowley said.

"Well, he should've," Elsa-May said flatly. "After what he did, he should've."

Crowley nodded. "It would've been easier to marry Sadie than to end up under a house."

"Well, once again we owe you many thanks, for helping Ettie with all these goings on," Elsa-May said.

"Yes, thank you. I don't know what I would've

done without you stepping in once that key was found. I haven't made a very good impression on Detective Kelly." Ettie ran her finger around the top of her teacup.

Crowley chuckled.

Ettie stared into her nettle tea. What would she do with Agatha's house? All those years of being a good friend to Agatha and she never breathed a word of what had happened to Horace. Then the scripture came to Ettie's mind: Luke 8:17. *For nothing is secret, that shall not be made manifest; neither any thing hid, that shall not be known and come abroad.*

"All secrets come home," Ettie muttered to herself while Crowley and Elsa-May reached as one for the last piece of cake.

* * * The End * * *

Thank you for your interest in
Secrets Come Home
Ettie Smith Amish Mysteries Book 1

* * * * * * * * * * * * *

For updates on
Samantha Price's new releases
and giveaways subscribe at:
http://www.samanthapriceauthor.com

If you liked this book
you might also enjoy
the ten book
Amish Secret Widows' Society series.
The Amish Widow Book 1

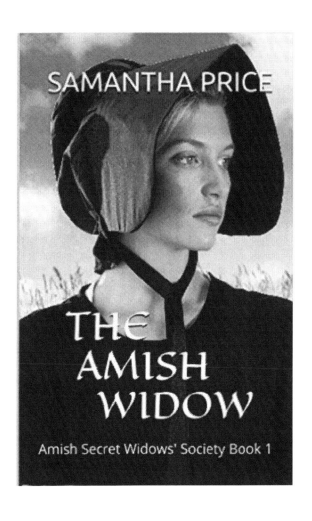

Newly widowed Amish woman Emma Kurtzler
has little time to grieve before she discovers that
someone is trying to force her from her farm.

The man who had the lease on her farm is found murdered shortly after informing Emma of his intention to break the lease.

In an effort to both save her farm and avoid becoming a suspect in the man's murder, Emma sets out to get to the bottom of things.

Emma befriends a group of Amish Widows and quickly discovers that there is more to these sweet Amish ladies than meets the eye when they willingly help her with her investigations.

In the midst of Emma's troubles she is drawn to Wil Jacobson, a friendly neighbor, but can she trust this man who is trying his best to win her heart?

* * * * * * * * * * * * *

Samantha Price loves to hear from her readers.
Connect with Samantha at:
samanthaprice333@gmail.com
http://twitter.com/AmishRomance
http://www.facebook.com/SamanthaPriceAuthor

50359230R00139

Made in the USA
Lexington, KY
12 March 2016